THE MEMORY BANK

THE MEMORY BANK

WALLACE WEST

WILDSIDE PRESS

CHAPTER 1

"When I need your advice, *Lieutenant* Commander," cooed the admiral, "I shall send you a plascript!"

"But sir," his husky, tow-headed aide ventured to protest, "Lieutenant Pancrief can make it right in the lab. It's just a refinement of an ancient sniper-scope. Infra-red radiations from the bodies of the Siriuns—if they have bodies, of course—would register on microfilm. They need never know…"

"Hah!" Admiral Mendez slammed a hairy fist on his empty desk top. "Can you keep those devils from reading your thoughts? I can't any more."

"They never probe the minds of non-depositors, sir. To be extra safe, though, Lieutenant Pancrief could build a thought scrambler. There's a description of a primitive one in a book I have."

"Books!" Mendez seemed about to spit. "Books have ruined more good C.S.N. men than have been killed by the barbarians. Stick to tri-di training films, Merek my boy." His bristle of moustache lifted in a smile. "Better chance of advancement that way."

"Yes sir," choked Merek.

"Let me brief you once more." The admiral spoke as to a naughty child. "We are guests of the Siriuns. We are seeking an alliance to combat aggression by the barbarians of Omega Centauri against the planets of Alpha, Beta and Proxima Centauri. If our hosts prefer to remain invisible it is good diplomacy to respect their wishes."

"How can we negotiate on even terms, sir, with beings no one has ever seen? Oh yes, Siriun merchant ships visit our star system. But no Centauran has ever seen, smelled or even touched a Siriun. We're working in the dark, both literally and figuratively. If you would only…"

"Sorry. I have my orders from the Merconian Council—and you have yours, sir. Dismissed!" Then, as his aide turned to leave the cabin, the admiral went completely out of character. "I can't have insubordination here, Merek," he almost pleaded as he rubbed stubby fingers across his forehead. "I haven't mentioned it before, but I'm a year overdue with my Memory Bank deposit. My mind is all cluttered up like an old attic. I've got to get this conference over with before I become senile. Please don't confuse me with those crazy ideas of yours. If you wish to present your proposal through the proper channels—seventeen copies and all that—I will see that it is forwarded to the Council."

"Where it will be pigeonholed, as you know, sir."

"Dismissed, I said!" roared the admiral. And, after Merek had squeezed through the doorway, he muttered: "Insolent young puppy. Can't be a day over fifty! Needs discipline. Yes, yes. Mustn't forget *that*! Discipline!" He made a note to consider the matter, then pulled himself together and started preparing for the next session with the Siriuns, which was only two hours away.

In his tiny cabin, Merek nursed a towering grouch and a forbidden bottle of Scopio while he considered tendering his resignation from the Centauran Space Navy. Nuh-uh! The Old Man wouldn't accept it. Had to have a whipping boy. He took a stiff drink and breached another rule by slitting a light-tight shutter and peering into the impenetrable darkness outside the flagship on the off-chance that he might catch a glimpse of a Siriun. His only reward was the sight of fluttery fog fingers pawing the heavy pane.

He closed the shutter with a wry grimace and reached automatically for one of the dog-eared, centuries-old books dealing with guerrilla warfare which lined the shelves he had built over his bunk. Then he shook his rough-hewn head and snapped the tri-di switch instead. If the Old Man wanted him to watch films, watch them he would—or watch *it*.

A two-foot-square shadow box in the cabin wall filled with misty light. The light solidified, took form as a room filled to the ceiling with panels of automatic calculators and Memory Bank indexes. A girl, dressed in a simple white chiton, sat on a chair of antique design in the center of that room. Bare feet primly crossed at their slim ankles, aristocratic hands folded, ash blonde hair piled in a coronet of braids above her broad forehead, Marian, Secretary of the Council which ruled the three habitable planets of the Alpha Centauri star system, was ready to give another of her famous lectures.

Merek made himself comfortable on the bunk, poured himself another drink and doused the lights so the tri-dimensional picture stood out in full depth and lifelike colors. The figure in the shadow box seemed to give the illusion of appearing, life size, before him. Its aloof beauty took his breath away. Almost a millennium old, they said—and still in the bloom of youth.

"Marian! Marian!" he sighed. "You would understand if I could talk to you instead of going through Mendez's confounded channels."

As if in answer, the girl's somewhat thin but perfectly chiseled lips parted, her bosoms rose proudly under the translucent silk and she began to speak in a voice compounded of distant bells and trumpets.

"Friends," she said, "let me tell you of the days when our glorious ancestors fled from dying Earth to find freedom on the planets of Centaurus. It is unfortunate that memories of those heroic times have had to be removed from the minds of Centaurans. Yet the old books are full of thrilling exploits of the Prime Generation and of the Second Generation to which I belong. We should all read those books without fail. They will make all of us proud that we are Centaurans—proud to defend our planets from barbarian attack and willing…"

There was a rap on the cabin door. Merek stopped the film, turned up the lights and dilated the opening.

A long man entered, a man so tall and lean he seemed two-dimensional.

"Got it!" chortled the newcomer with a great bobbing of his Adam's apple. He held out a lean hand on which reposed a C.S.N. uniform button.

"Got what?" yawned Merek, resealing the door and waving toward the bottle.

"Your super-sniperscope. Just finished it. Substitute it for a regulation button, get within a hundred feet of a Siriun and you'll be able to determine whether he shaved this morning when you develop the film."

"Thanks, Pancrief," said Merek with a wry grin, "but the Old Man says 'No!'"

"You going to take it lying down?"

"What else? He's just waiting for a chance to break me."

"Um!" Pancrief tossed the button on the bed. "Well, it's not my funeral but I do think someone around here should do something besides chin with spooks. I might add that it would take a smart spook to detect that sniperscope."

His roving eye fell upon the shadow box where Marian's image sat immobile, washed out and vaguely accusing, her pretty mouth open.

"Didn't know I was interrupting a tryst," he winked. "Pray continue."

"Nuts," said his friend, but he cut the lights and started the film.

"…to fight to the death to defend our way of life," the Council Secretary resumed exactly where she had left off.

"That old rabble rouser," groaned Pancrief. "If you must listen to the witch, why not get some of her scientific lectures? They're good. But this patriotic blather…phooey!"

"Happens to be the only one of her talks aboard." Merek sat up so quickly he banged his head on the low ceiling. "As for your calling Marian a…"

"Excuse me. Excuse me. I meant no disrespect to Her Intelligence. But let me warn you in all seriousness, pal, that mooning over the Council Secretary is a waste of time. You're not in her class; not while you have to wipe the Old Man's nose every time he sneezes."

Pancrief left quickly, and Merek switched off the tri-di, turned up the lights and started pacing the cabin. Three steps forward… Turn… Three steps back… Turn… He had been doing that for a solid year now, ever since the flagship *Alpha* had landed and the interminable conferences had begun. The whole of the Dark Planet was off-limits to Centaurans.

Pancrief was right, he thought. Besides being handicapped by his youth, and kept in virtual poverty by his lack of Memory Bank dividends, Merek was cordially detested by his Second Generation admiral because he dared make suggestions.

The button on the bed caught his eye. He picked the thing up. A work of art, he decided, like all of Pancriefs gadgets, with an almost invisible switch on the rim to start and stop the camera hidden inside. He started to drop it in the waste chute, then hesitated. He hadn't much to lose; the Old Man would get him sooner or later. The conference with the Siriuns was scheduled to resume in 40 minutes. With fingers that trembled slightly, he twisted a button off his uniform jacket and substituted the super-sniperscope.

* * * *

Every light on the flagship blinked out as conference time approached. The main port was unsealed and opened upon the gray nothingness outside. A guard of honor commanded by Merek lined up stiffly at attention along the pitch-black gangway leading to Admiral Mendez's quarters.

"We are here, puny human!"

The words were not spoken. They grated like rusty needles on the cortex of Merek's brain. He saluted and escorted the whispers into the conference room, where Mendez stood sweating and uncomfortable behind his empty desk. Then he unlimbered his pocket steno, preparatory to taking notes on the meeting.

"Despicable Centauran," the needle skittered at Mendez, "we have consulted our…superiors. Your proposals for an alliance with us are beneath contempt!"

"But why, Your Magnificence?" the admiral's rasping voice shattered the stillness of the room. "You have a profitable trade with the Centauran planets as the result of the treaty which you and I negotiated hundreds of years ago. That trade will be lost if the barbarians conquer Centaurus. Emperor Rolph and his wild men despise all luxuries; if they seize the resources of Mercon, Arcon and Pizar, they will have no need for your wares."

"True," grated a second needle, rustier and blunter than the first, "but we Siriuns can wait. As they become civilized the barbarians will learn to value Siriun luxuries as much as you do. But you are decadent while they are members of a more virile human strain; therefore they will breed and multiply as you do not. Soon their requirements for Siriun goods will exceed yours. To put it bluntly, Sirius stands to profit greatly by your extermination."

"But—but it was you Siriuns who originally forced the Centauran planets to limit their populations. That stipulation is in our trade treaty."

"True," screeched the thought of the first Siriun like a fingernail drawn across tin, "but circumstances have altered. Shall we conclude this ridiculous conference, worm?"

Realizing that time had suddenly begun to run out, Merek brushed a hand across the breast of his tunic.

"Wait, Your Magnificence!" By heroic effort Mendez managed to ignore the Siriun's studied insult. "The Council authorizes me to enlarge our offer. If there is an alliance, Centaurus will reveal to you the secret of its Memory Bank."

"That thought was in your mind when you arrived here," mocked Needle #2. "Why have you not voiced it before?"

"Well, uh…" The admiral wished once again that he had made his Bank deposit on schedule; his overcrowded brain was churning like the Coal Sack. "Centaurans, uh, like to bargain. I…"

"Something is amiss!" Needle #1 jabbed. "I sense danger!"

"What, Your Magnificence?" gasped the admiral as Merek adjusted his tie.

"I do not know. Let it pass. Our…superiors will want to consider your Memory Bank offer for ten sleeps. Await our return." The needlers departed without further ceremony, like gusts of night wind.

As soon as he had presumably ushered out their visitors, sealed the port and turned on the ship's lights, Merek headed for the micro-lab. As he expected, he found the gangling Pancrief puttering there. He handed over the button without comment. Moments later its 1/2-mm film was in a pan of developer. Minutes later the two conspirators stared blankly at a uniformly fogged thread of plastic.

"Over-exposed," snarled Merek, tossing it aside.

"No!" Pancrief grabbed the film and held it under a magnifier. "Double exposed! There's something—or some things—here." He pointed to a smudge which appeared on each frame. "Our ghostics are smarter than I thought. They managed to fog the film right in the camera."

"Or in the developing tank!" Merek looked over his shoulder. "How do we know they left the ship?"

"Guess you're younger than we think!" Pancrief fumbled at a cigarette.

A squawk-box in the laboratory ceiling sputtered: "Lieutenants Merek and Pancrief. Report to admiral's quarters at once!"

"'Lieutenants,'" sighed Pancrief. "The brig yawns for us."

It was a gray but thoroughly furious Mendez who faced them. Having just received a nasty kicking, he was bent on passing it along.

"The Siriuns have communicated with me by radio," he barked. "They ask your immediate deportation. Anything to say?"

"Only that the sniperscope film was fogged in some way," Merek answered. "We got no pictures, sir."

Mendez was not placated. "So you made a monkey out of me for nothing," he raged. "Insubordination...plus inefficiency. A disgrace to the service. Each of you is reduced one grade." He lunged around the desk and ripped a stripe off their sleeves. "A Siriun ship leaves for Pizar at 2100. You will be on board. When you reach Pizar..."

"*If* we reach Pizar, sir," Merek corrected.

"If you reach Pizar, report to Rear Admiral Patterson for further disciplining. That is all...except that punishment for second offenses will be dishonorable discharge and withdrawal of Memory Bank privileges. Dismissed!"

CHAPTER II

Merek and Pancrief remembered nothing of the trip back to Centaurus. They were put under suspended animation, not only to conserve precious food and air but to keep them from spying out any Siriun secrets. How much time did the journey require? Well, that is always a moot question at faster-than-light speeds. Viewed from a fixed point in space, the Sirius-Centaurus hop probably consumed quite a number of years. But, since there are no fixed spatial points, time aboard the ship slowed down in exact ratio to a similar slowing down of clocks on Centaurus. (According to the Lorentz transformation, there can be no possible distinction between the speed of the ship and the speed of the home planet, which may be said with equal justice to be rushing toward it.) The end result was that the subjective time elapsed on a flight several light years long usually was only a matter of weeks to all concerned.

But the two did not concern themselves with paradoxes when they recovered consciousness to find themselves lying on the chilly pavement of Pizar City spaceport. Almost blinded by the wan light of little Proxima, they stood up groggily and squinted about in search of the Naval Base building. Finally they had to ask directions from a group of servo-mechanisms which had shoved the end of a portable conveyor into the globe of darkness which was the Siriun ship and were waiting to receive the gossamer laces, light-as-air fabrics and other exquisite artifacts as they came sliding down the belt.

"Sunshine!" sighed Pancrief as he lit a cigarette and drew a deep, pure breath of smoke. "God, it's good to be home and in sunshine, even if home is only a second-rate planet. Another month of murk would have made me as crazy as the Old Man."

"What kind of chap is Patterson?" Merek asked as they started off toward the base.

"Pizarian, of course. No love lost between him and Mendez."

"Be seated, gentlemen," the rear admiral said civilly enough when they stumbled into his office. "I have received a message from Admiral Mendez regarding your breach of discipline. Tsk! Tsk!" A frosty twinkle showed in world-weary gray eyes. "He asks that I discipline you further. Ahem!" He pulled at a long nose. "The only way I can do that is to restore you to your former ranks and work you to death."

They goggled at him.

"You'll have a 24-hour-a-day job," Patterson snapped. "The base is undermanned. I have ten out-of-date cruisers with which to protect the whole planet. One of them, the *Shark*, is grounded for overhaul. You will report to her Captain Penn at once.

"What you tried to do out on Sirius was commendable, in my worthless opinion as a Pizarian. Let us say no more about the matter—except that if I ran to the Council before I made every move, Pizar would have been in barbarian hands a year ago.

"One thing more, gentlemen. You are to be my guests at the Planetary Ball tonight. Report here at 20 hours. No thanks, please. You are dismissed."

* * * *

"Velvet," Pancrief sighed several hours later as he draped his lank body over a bunk in the double cabin to which they had been assigned by Captain Penn. "I can't understand it."

"I can." Merek was removing the beard which had grown during their period of unconsciousness. "Did you take a look 'round the port?"

"Looks no different than when I left here five years ago. Discipline a bit lax, but we Pizarians are like that. Comes of being the orphans of the system."

"The place is just begging for trouble. It's on peacetime footing."

"Who'd bother with Pizar?" Pancrief dragged himself partially erect and reached for the tube of depilatory. "The only real Centauran wealth is on Mercon and Arcon."

"How about women?"

"'Pizarian girls are fair as pearls,'" Pancrief quoted. "So what?"

"Come off it, Pan! You know Rolph's barbarians are hard up for wives. I don't quite know why; perhaps some factor in the environment out in Omega favors male births. Already they've made three minor raids on Pizar. Meantime most of our fleet is guarding Mercon and Arcon. We've landed on a powder keg."

"Maybe we'll see some action at last."

"If you were a barbarian," said Merek, "and you wanted to snatch the prettiest and most dissatisfied women on Pizar, where and when would you stage a big raid?"

Pancrief stopped toweling the whiskers off his face. "I'd raid the plush Planetary Ball tonight."

"Quite!" Merek buckled on his dress sword and automatic. "Let's go talk to Captain Penn about this."

The captain, a jovial little man with a high opinion of his commanding officer, was not greatly impressed.

"We have thought of the danger and taken all steps to meet it," he chuckled. "The ballroom will be surrounded by a double cordon of our best men. Two cruisers will be overhead at all times and two others will be on the alert as they patrol nearby."

"What if the barbarians try to infiltrate the ball?" asked Merek. "Have you ever met a barbarian?"

"When I was in college I knew one pretty well. He was…"

"They stand out like sore thumbs," Penn interrupted. "The few I've seen actually smelled." He tapped a perfumed handkerchief to his nose. "And they talk the most outlandish jargon. Even if they put on civilized clothing you could spot them a mile off."

"You don't think we should remain on board tonight, sir?"

"No use. She won't be spaceworthy till tomorrow. No. You come along with me. The admiral is waiting." Penn straightened his sword, adjusted his cap to just the right angle and led the way.

Little Pizar outdid itself for its one important social event of the year. A poor planet, whose inhabitants devoted themselves mainly to agriculture and to space shipbuilding, it went all out tonight in an effort to show that it bowed to neither Mercon or Arcon. As they zoomed across town in Patterson's flying limousine they could see that the streets were festooned with lights and that those not fortunate enough to get invitations to the ball itself were holding their own dances in less imposing buildings.

"What a set-up," Pancrief whispered in Merek's ear.

With some difficulty they found parking space on the roof of the governor's mansion. They descended the stairs to the main ballroom, making the most of their white, skintight uniforms, gold braid and clinking swords. All about them rose a sea of handsome faces, but Merek had never seen so many sulky, prettily-pouting girls in one place in his life.

"What's the matter with your countrywomen?" he asked Pancrief. "Most of them look mad enough to bite nails."

"Envy is gnawing at their sweet vitals," the other grinned. "Mercon's Planetary Ball last year was held on a specially-constructed platform floating above the capital. One of the seven ballrooms was equipped with anti-gravs so tired couples could float to music and rest their dogs. Pizar can't afford to put on a show like that."

"It would serve them right if the barbarians did come," said Merek.

"I suspect that some of the girls feel that way too."

Governor Price, son of the founder of Pizar's First Family, greeted them effusively at the bottom of the stairs. His wife, whose eyes were too bright and whose lips were too red, and who wore a tiny live lizard on the shoulder of her scarlet dress, seized upon Patterson, scolded him for being late and swept him out on the floor. Her leggy daughter made off with Captain Penn. Merek and Pancrief gravitated toward the bar and found places under the life-size, smiling tri-di photographs of President Franklin and Secretary Marian of the Council.

They ordered Scopio instead of their usual beer. Merek automatically lifted his glass to the lovely creature looking down on him.

"Merek, my son," said Pancrief, "I wish you would forget that dame on the wall and look about you for a partner amongst the beauty and, to put it politely, the youth of Pizar."

"They eat persimmons," grunted the commander.

"True, but they have their points."

"Yes, I must admit that this new fad for ancient Greek draperies is better than the one which was in vogue when I was at school."

"The time when people tried to look like robots and to make robots which looked like people," chuckled Pancrief. "That was bad."

"Another fad seems to be aborning," said Merek. "Notice how many girls have brought pets to the ball. There's a girl with a parrot on her shoulder."

"That one has a hamster…and her companion has a white mouse. Brrr! I'd rather have my Pizarian girls neat. They lose their inhibitions after a few drinks, incidentally."

"Let 'em keep 'em," said Merek, looking from face to lovely face and not liking what he found there. Was it, he pondered, that they had lived too long—and too well—despite their wails of poverty? Was the boon of almost everlasting life a curse in disguise?

"How does that one strike you?" Pancrief jogged his elbow.

Merek looked and drew breath through his teeth. Not ten feet from him stood a girl! She was tall, all of six feet. Her blue-black hair curled in ringlets about a head which a sculptor would have envied. There was a faint bridge of freckles across a retrousse nose. Her mouth was generously large. Her chin had a dimple. Her throat was round and deeply tanned in contrast to the milk-white women about her. Her shoulders were those of a swimmer, rising defiantly from a topless black silk sheath. Her…

"Now, now!" warned Pancrief, whose eyes nevertheless continued traveling leisurely downward, noticing the incongruous white rabbit under her arm, the flat stomach, slim hips, long legs and, indeed, every inch of the vision down to the gold cords which bound her dancing sandals to perfect ankles.

"Who is she?" breathed Merek as the girl tossed back her head and laughed—actually laughed—at something a burly escort had said.

"Haven't the faintest. I'd remember that face. Visiting celebrity, perhaps. I'd say a Second Gen because of that scar."

"Scar?" Merek looked again and noticed that a thin red line crossed the girl's left shoulder and breast.

"Let's introduce us," said Pancrief, putting down his empty glass. "Her escort can't take offense. Informality's the password tonight."

Before he could move, the orchestra struck up an old waltz. The girl and her partner were swept away by the strains.

"Lot of faces here I don't recognize," said Pancrief two drinks later. "That tall redhead…and that fellow with the teeth and the grin. You don't find many such grins on Pizar."

"He's making quite a hit with the ladies," Merek agreed. "Notice. He's drifting from one to another and whispering to perfect strangers… Oh, oh! That one slapped him!"

"Party's getting rough," said Pancrief. "I've been to a lot of these balls and I never heard such a racket. Listen."

Merek nodded. There was something here which was out of the ordinary, a rising surge of devil-may-care revelry unusual among the staid Centaurans of this highly civilized age. Most of the women were losing their inhibitions all right.

"Notish anything odd about this liquor?" asked Pancrief.

"It's twisting your tongue. We'd better find partners and dance."

"I dance with nobody but the tall redhead."

"O.K. There she is with the girl who has the scar. They're talking to the orchestra leader."

Merek started pushing his way through the mob. It was tough going. He was only half way across the floor when the music stopped with a crash of cymbals and roll of drums.

"L-ladies and gentlemen," the pallid bandmaster spoke into his invisible microphone. "Silence, please. I have an important announcement." The din decreased a few degrees. "I have been a-asked to tell you that this is a raid. Barbarians are amongst us…"

A roar of laughter interrupted him. Merek, with Pan close behind him, stood frozen.

"No. No. Please. This is no joke," pleaded the orchestra leader. "A raiding party of 500 barbarians has infiltrated the hall… I have just been given proof…"

"Nonsense!" Patterson and the governor had mounted part way up the stairs. "Look about you. Do you see anyone faintly resembling a filthy barbarian? This is a bad joke. My men are guarding every entrance and exit of this building." Catching sight of Merek and Pancrief, he thundered: "Officers. Arrest that bandmaster. He's a saboteur."

A man and woman in faultless evening dress ran up the stairs, automatics in hand. The governor and the admiral lifted their hands; were herded from sight.

"Grab the girl with the scar," yelped Pancrief. "I'll take the redhead. We've got to get them out of here before they get hurt."

He lunged forward and was met by a straight-arm jab which slammed him back against the bandstand so hard that his teeth rattled. Before he could recover, redhead had vanished in the crowd.

Merek snatched at the other girl. She eluded him and started wriggling through the press in the direction of the kitchens. As the mob thinned somewhat he was almost upon her. Quick as a cat she whirled, winked sardonically, and tossed her pet rabbit into his face.

Merek dodged by reflex action, knocking the flying creature out of his path. He started forward again, then stopped with a yell and began flailing at his legs.

"What's the matter?" Pancrief shouted as he galloped up.

Merek turned on him a face in which shock struggled with horror.

"The rabbit!" he gulped. "The damned rabbit—bit me on the leg!"

They looked around for the girl with the scar. She wasn't there. Behind them the voice of the orchestra leader continued its pleading: "Nobody will be hurt if he follows directions... Ladies to the south side of the room. Gentlemen to the north. Throw all weapons into the middle of the floor... Naughty!" There was the sound of a shot. "Sorry that had to happen, ladies and gentlemen... That's better... Hold your hands high..."

Their spines creeping in expectation that bullets would follow them, Merek and Pancrief plunged through an open diaphragm into the kitchens, dodged various servos, and located a service exit. Dashing down flights of seldom-used stairs, they finally reached the gardens surrounding the mansion.

"I'll alert the guard," panted Pancrief.

"Save your breath," Merek ordered. "If shooting starts here, there will be a slaughter. The only thing we can try to do is keep the barbs from getting back to their ships. Head for the *Shark*."

Using moving sidewalks where they could, springing across town where they had to, they succeeded in reaching the port's outskirts.

"Take it easy," whispered Merek. "The place may be surrounded."

But the sentry reported no disturbance.

"No, Captain Penn has not returned. A raid?" He stared. "Impossible. Why..."

"Take us to the control tower at once!" Merek cut off his ramblings.

The squad car screamed across the thousand-acre field. In the tower they found a frantic C.O. tearing his hair.

"Static!" he gabbled at the newcomers. "Static on FM! Can't be. But there it is. I've lost contact with all the cruisers... A raid, you say. Impossible!"

They left him dithering; screeched across the field once more to where the *Shark* lay helpless on her cradle, routed out her skeleton crew and then did a bit of dithering themselves.

"Is there any way to get this piece of junk into the air?" Merek yelled at the pajama-clad and blinking chief engineer when he and other officers assembled on the bridge.

"Impossible, sir. Her main tubes are down."

"How about her anti-gravs?" Pancrief asked.

"Well, uh, they're only for take-off and landing. I could lift her ten miles or so with them, but it's risky. Unless Captain Penn ordered it, sir, I couldn't take the responsibility." He squared his shoulders.

Merek drew a long breath. "Captain Penn is either dead or a prisoner," he answered levelly. "I'm in command here. Take her up at once, directly over the port, as high as she'll go."

The engineer, a Pizarian, sized up his new commander. Then he said, "Yes sir," saluted briskly and marched out.

"Nice going," said Pancrief out of the corner of his mouth.

"Lieutenant Pancrief will act as my aide," Merek said to the *Shark's* trio of officers. "We won't be able to move rapidly but we may be able to give a good account of ourselves till help comes. You…" he nodded to the deck officers, "put the fear of High Barbary into the crew. You—I'm sorry I don't know your name yet—break out the flasher and try to contact any cruisers nearby. Use the interplanetary transmitter to alert Mercon. Keep sending, whether you get through or not. Lieutenant Pancrief, take over the guns and shoot anything that moves. I'll man the controls, such as they are."

The engine room telltale blinked and Merek signaled for elevation. A screen above the control board brightened, giving them a full view of the night sky lighted faintly by the twin suns of Alpha and Beta Centauri near the southern horizon. The C.O. began tapping out dots and dashes on the blinker key. The radio receiver chattered with static.

Slowly, waveringly, the *Shark* began pushing herself away from the surface of Pizar. Up and up she went until she hovered on invisible stilts ten miles in the stratosphere. As she went up, the static diminished to a distant howl.

"Hello the *Shark*," a worried voice spoke over this background noise. "This is the *Tiger*. Commander Pleines speaking. Can you hear me? Over."

"The *Bream* here," came a different voice. "Commander Pritchard. Over."

Merek outlined the situation to the other cruisers. "Any barb ships sighted?" he ended.

"Not a pip on the radar till you came up," Pleines reported. "Nothing but static from the ground. They must have sneaked in low under that. Over."

"Check," said Pritchard.

A faint voice spoke up, ghostly on the darkened bridge.

"Commander Pitkin of the *Partridge* reporting," it said. "We're coming in but it will take us an hour to get there. I have relayed your information to the other cruisers. They're all heading for Pizar City. Meantime, if Commanders Pleines and Pritchard approve, I suggest that, since you know most about what happened downstairs, you take command, sir."

The Pizarians were passing the buck, as they always did when a Merconian shoulder was handy to lean on. "Very well. Stand by for orders."

He studied the situation below through the infra-red magniscope. A procession of some kind was being moved along Pizar City's main boulevard, heading south toward a group of wooded hills. Scanning its apparent destination, he found nothing unusual there—just a small suburb of modernistic cottages, laid out in neat rows on a meadow through which a brook meandered.

Walking the *Shark* ponderously on its miles-high stilts, he searched an area 20 miles in diameter for evidences of an enemy landing.

"Lieutenant Pancrief," he said at last, "will you take a look at this?"

Pan scanned the plate for long moments, then shook his tousled head.

"Same old hick town," he grunted. "Looks just as it did when I was last home on furlough, except for that new suburb. Lord, what will those crazy architects be making people live in next?" He slouched back to his calculator.

Merek studied the procession. It was long enough to include not only the invading barbarians but every woman who had attended the ball.

He bit his lip. It seemed impossible that whoever was in command down there didn't know that three Centauran ships were watching them. Yet there was no attempt at concealment and complete contempt for the tens of thousands of Pizarians who must be snarling with fury.

Well, what could he or they do about it? Neither dared attack for fear of killing the captives.

"Say," exclaimed Pancrief as he stole another glance through the 'scope. (The procession had poured off the terminus of the moving way and was now marching across the meadow.) "You don't suppose the barbs have decided to stay on Pizar, do you?"

"Get back to your post!" yelled Merek. "Here they come!"

Pancrief jabbed commands into the gun sighter as a great globe shot into view out of Alpha's glare. It was coming at such speed that, even in the thin stratosphere, its metal skin glowed cherry red.

The calculator whirred. Streaks of radiation flashed simultaneously from the turrets of the three cruisers, setting the air blazing in their wake. The first stabs were wild. Within seconds, they steadied and crept in for a bull's-eye.

But their target didn't oblige! It swerved madly, saw it couldn't escape those questing fingers…and vanished into thin air ten miles to the northwest.

"Got him the first time!" Merek pounded Pancrief on his bony back.

"Got him nothing! Didn't come within a mile of him. And they've got a fix on us now. Move!"

Merek dropped the *Shark* a thousand feet, slamming himself and the others hard against the ceiling of the bridge. Even as he did so another cherry red globe whizzed over the horizon, three rays blazing. One missed the dropping *Shark* and another the zigzagging *Tiger*. But the *Bream* had not moved quickly enough; it exploded as the infra-heat struck it squarely amidships.

Pancrief had been ready for this attack. Two of the *Shark's* rays grazed the hurtling globe. It vanished as before but one huge white hot melting section of it remained in view. Turning slowly, this fragment followed the dead *Bream*.

"What in hell's name are those things?" shouted the C.O.

"Barb ships," said Merek through his teeth. "The next one's got our number on it. Hold on!" He managed to cling to his chair as he sent the cruiser zooming to the limit of its anti-gravs.

"Maybe not," panted the C.O. "Here come reinforcements." His screen was suddenly alive with speeding pips.

Nevertheless the globes tried again. The *Tiger* went down in flaming ruin but the enemy calculators evidently could not grasp the fact that the *Shark* was operating entirely on anti-gravs and therefore failed to chart her bobbing course. Not only did they miss her consistently but one of their globes was caught in Pancrief's broadside and melted to a puddle.

The enemy called it quits at that point; no more of them appeared. On points, it seemed a clean-cut victory for the lighter home team. Score: Two cruisers against one battleship lost and one damaged.

Eventually Merek found time to look toward the ground once more. "Pan," he said hoarsely. "Come here. I must be going blind."

His friend peered into the plate, then gulped convulsively. "Gone!" he marveled. "That new suburb has plumb disappeared."

"Suburb! That was another barb ship!"

"And while the others were playing tag with us, it took off with about 5,000 of the prettiest women in the universe," sighed Pancrief. "Too bad. I would have liked to get acquainted with that redhead!"

"But how?" mourned the Merconian. "How could what looked like a group of summer cottages be a ship? It doesn't make sense."

"We'll find out…if we live long enough," said Pan, lighting a cigarette in defiance of regulations. "Meantime, let's go downstairs, have several stiff drinks and take our punishment."

CHAPTER III

"*Good* morning, Admiral Mendez." The teller with the blonde voice smiled across her desk at the man with five comets on his uniform. "Time for your deposit *already*? Goodness! How the decades fly."

"I'm past due, Mrs. Millston." His body remained taut.

"Oh dear. That *is* unfortunate. There's a penalty for tardiness, you know; a rather stiff one." She consulted her calculator and frowned prettily. "Of course, you *have* accumulated quite a dividend during the past eleven years. We might charge the penalty off against *that*."

He flinched at her repeated emphasis and began to perspire. "I have an excuse, Miss Milestone."

Goodness, he *is* in a state, thought the teller.

"My delay is due to The Trouble," he bumbled. "I have been on an official mission to…seeking allies in…" He gulped. "The name of the star system evades me just at the moment but I have it in file of course. It was impossible to return earlier, also…"

"Yes, Admiral?" she coaxed as his slab-sided face reddened.

"Well, dammit, if you *must* know: My present wife has run up bills on the strength of those accumulated dividends. If they're wiped out…"

"What a pity." The clerk tapped her teeth with the end of a stylus, then brightened. "Do you have an *official* excuse, Admiral?"

"Oh yes. I had forg… I mean, I have it here somewhere." He finally produced a long envelope and presented it with fingers that shook.

"Well, *now* I'm sure everything can be arranged. I'll speak to the manager." She rose with conscious grace. "Just make yourself comfortable, Admiral. You'll have time for a run-through before the booth is ready."

"Thank you, Miss Midston." He crumpled into a chair and stared straight before him. A run-through? There wasn't much worth remembering. Perhaps the time he had won his fifth comet. That had been…let's see… That had been in 2908…or was it 2909?… Some trouble with the Pizarians?… The memory eluded him. Why bother? He shook his head, then sat in a kind of trance until Mrs. Minton returned.

"*Everything* has been arranged, Admiral," she cooed, patting his shoulder. "The manager says there need be no penalty this time." She ushered him through an inner door, sat down at her desk and stared at the wall in her turn.

"There, but for the grace of God, and The Bank, go I," she murmured with a shrug that was half shudder. Briskly she began punching at her calculator.

An hour later Admiral Mendez came back through the door. He was stiff as a new ramrod now. "My receipt, please, Mrs. Minton," he snapped and added, "I'm sure you're too discreet to remember my maunderings."

"Of course, sir." She was all business. "Your next deposit is due ten years from today. That's June 28, 3012." He still refused to unbend, so she added, "Don't forget to be prompt. The Bank cannot accept a second excuse."

* * * *

Mendez marched briskly along the broad and winding belt of turf which was Mercon City's main thoroughfare. Spring was in the winy air. Alpha Centauri and its companion sun were well up in a sky spangled with lazy clouds, but so clear that little Proxima could be seen sparkling faintly near the western horizon.

Meadowlarks from far-distant Earth, and a host of flying things native to Mercon, were singing in trees so densely blossomed that they half-hid the city's neo-Hellenic buildings. Stately men in brief tunics and calm, large-eyed women dressed in diaphanous, vari-colored robes, walked barefoot in and out of the theaters, stores and gracious dwellings. Once he even saw a child with its mother. (That meant good luck.) It was good to be alive and whole again.

Or was it? The space dog's steps lagged. He was in for a bad time at the Capitol. He would have to report that his trip had been one long nightmare of frustration. If only he could have banked *that* memory!

But Marian would worm every detail out of him, even if it took all of this lovely day when he had hoped to go fishing.

Dawdle as he might, the ninety broad marble steps eventually loomed ahead. He mounted each one as if it had been a scaffold. Yet there was a curious excitement within him. All men felt it when they approached Her Intelligence. A scrap of thousand-year-old poetry drifted through his mind:

> *A daughter of the gods, divinely tall,*
> *And most divinely fair.*

"A daughter of devils, rather," Mendez snarled.

He passed down a wide corridor, exchanging greetings with a number of passing notables and entered a vast, simply decorated and softly lighted room. Its walls were lined to the ceiling with plastic-and-glass panels behind which, Mendez thought with a touch of awe, were the memories of

Marian's lifetime, waiting to be brought back to consciousness at the zip of a switch. If *he* had his own one hundred deposits available like that, instead of stuck off in the stacks of the bank somewhere, the admiral grumbled internally, *he* might be able to make good use of them, too, on occasion!

The mistress of this fantastic library was seated, primly erect in an unupholstered chair of antique design, near a window overlooking the Capitol gardens. Her high-arched, perfectly manicured feet were primly crossed on a footstool. Her fine lips were compressed into a thin line. Yet, despite her evident anger, she managed to be heartbreakingly beautiful with her masses of ash-blonde hair bound high in the old Greek way, her silken-lashed blue eyes and her figure…

"I trust you bring success with you, Mendez," she interrupted his musings with a voice like a 'cello as she held out a slim left hand to be kissed. (If his trip had been successful, he knew, she would have offered her right.)

"You know I don't," he rasped. "Those go…" He bit his tongue. "Those Siriuns won't play!"

"Play, Mendez?"

"You know what I mean. They looked through me and telepathed that Mercon was done for, washed up and flushed down the drain."

"Old English slang offends me." Somehow, she managed to frown without creasing her perfect forehead.

"Siriuns offend *me*, shoving their slimy thoughts into my brain like—like rusty needles. They hate everyone, including themselves, I believe."

"Why won't they cooperate?"

Why, he thought, did this woman have to be so *efficiently* beautiful?

"First," he answered, "because we're an alien race to them. Second, because they have a life span of only twenty or so of our years."

"Did you tell them we would make them almost immortal if they joined us against the barbarians?"

"I did. They said I lied."

"Lied?" She leaned forward to shoot the word at him. He forced himself to look away from the charms displayed by that sudden movement.

"Yes," he managed to say carefully, "the Siriuns said we lied for two reasons. The first was that, since theirs is a rapidly expanding civilization, we would never dare give them the secret of longevity. If we did, we eventually would have to fight not only the hordes of barbarians from Omega, as we are now doing, but we would have to guard our rear against an overwhelming number of Siriuns. They say nobody, even a decadent human, could be that stupid."

"And the second reason?" She was biting her lips now.

"They said we couldn't give them immortality because they wouldn't accept it."

"I don't understand." Her pale, heart-shaped face lost its composure.

"Neither do I. They seem to think an extremely long life span saps the vitality of a race and they want none of it. Incidentally, that's why they contend we cannot hold out against the barbs."

"Nonsense." She rose and paced the room in a swirl of draperies.

"So I told them. I pointed out that our defenses are impregnable; our numbers overwhelming; our weapons immeasurably superior to Rolph's. I said The Bank supplies us with an almost unlimited fund of knowledge… Well, have you ever tried to reason with a Siriun? If not, don't!"

"Then your trip to Sirius was a complete failure, Mendez?"

"I achieved our minimum objective, Intelligence," he replied stiffly. "The Siriuns agree to sell us supplies if…"

"…If we guarantee them one hundred percent net profit on every transaction, over and above any loss or damage to their merchant ships. Is that it?"

"How did you know?" He stared at her, deflated.

"I know you!" She resumed her seat. "But do *you* know what the barbarians did yesterday to our impregnable defenses?"

"I—uh—wasn't at the office. What did they do?"

"Fishing again, eh?" Her eyes snapped fire. "They raided Pizar and stole five thousand of our women."

"The devils!"

"I suspect the women they kidnapped have another word for them." She smiled bitterly. "Have you ever stopped to think, Mendez, what may be the subconscious yearnings of a healthy woman who is permitted to have a child only once a century?"

"Well, no." He actually blushed. "Can't say as I have."

"Do so, some time. Then you may understand why the Siriuns think we're, what is it? 'flushed down the drain.' But that's not my point. If it hadn't been for the quick thinking of Captain Merek, we might have lost the entire planet of Pizar. And Pizar is too close to Mercon and Arcon for comfort."

"Merek? Merek?" The admiral stared at his manicured finger nails. "But he is a commander, not a captain. What did he do?"

"His commanding officer was attending a ball at the Pizarian capital and got himself scooped up, along with the women. Merek put our ships into the air, caught the raiders on the ground and forced them to retreat."

"Excellent. Excellent. Shows you how quickly the Admiralty can issue an order."

"*Captain* Merek didn't wait for an order. He acted on his own initiative."

"That's rank insubordination. I'll have the puppy broken for it."

"Will you, Mendez?" There were knives in her voice.

"Certainly. Orders must go through channels."

"And if they had, what would have happened to Pizar? We'd have lost it."

"Are you implying that the Admiralty is inefficient?"

"Not implying!" She sprang to her feet, glorious eyes ablaze. "Admiral Mendez, these are your orders…through channels—the channels of the Council of Merconian Savants of which I am chairman. You have two years in which to smash the barbarians; to drive them back to Omega. I don't care how you do it, but *do it*! Otherwise you will be relieved from duty and replaced by that 'puppy' Merek, who has won Mercon its only real victory since the barbarians started infiltrating."

If apoplexy had not been a forgotten disease, Mendez would have died from it, then and there. Eventually he got himself under control and his color returned to normal. His broad face became canny. "And when I succeed," he said, "what dividend will The Bank pay me?"

"Anything you ask, I presume. What do you want?"

"You!"

"You insolent dog!" The pale roses in her cheeks burned to crimson. "You're already married."

"My marriage occurred ninety years ago. It will be cancelled automatically when I make my next deposit. I can wait that long, Marian."

"Well…" Some of her anger faded as she studied him coolly. "I might do worse, I suppose. The people are becoming a bit concerned about my long celibacy."

"And the records say you were my first wife," he pointed out slyly.

"Yes. I know." She shook her head in puzzlement. "You must have been far different in your youth, Mendez. I can't say that you are my ideal now."

"Ideal!" he snorted. "You talk like a child instead of the second ranking leader of the Centauran Confederacy. And as for change, we've all changed for the better as the result of living a thousand years or so. I've delved into the printed records of my past. Just before leaving for Sirius I even went through the red tape necessary to withdraw and scan my very first Bank deposit in the hope that it would remind me how to deal with primitive peoples."

"And did it?" She regarded him with new interest.

"Of course not. I remembered leading a bayonet charge against the panic-stricken Merconian natives—I was just a lieutenant then, and a J.G. at that. Hand-to-hand combat. Buckets of blood. Tattered flags flying. Yells. Screams of agony. Pfui! It turned my stomach. Now we fight only at long range with the clean fire of radiation cannon. No dead bodies. No blood.

Not even any pain. That's progress, Marian. Real progress!"

"Is it?" Her face had a haunted look. "Sometimes I think that the Sirians are right when they call it decadence. Sometimes I think that we of the Second Generation have progressed so far that we have lost touch with reality, just as we have lost touch with our own past. Perhaps the future, in this time of change, belongs to young, uninhibited people like your Captain Merek."

"Young!" Mendez beat his broad chest till it resounded like a drum. "I'm as good a man as I ever was, even though I was born just after the old Centaurus left Earth in '99." As she smiled at him, unconvinced, he changed the painful subject. "How long since you had a husband, Marian?"

"So long that I've forgotten." She passed a hand across her face as though brushing away a cobweb. "My statement says a hundred and thirty years."

"No wonder the people are grumbling. It's time you had another child."

"If the barbarians raid Mercon, that may be no problem." She laughed without mirth and turned to the keyboard of her personal calculator to indicate the interview was ended. Over a dimpled shoulder she added: "We'll talk about this again, Mendez—when you return as a conquering hero."

CHAPTER IV

Spurred on by Marian's half-promise, the admiral did his best. He broke all his fishing poles. He went daily to a gym and lost three inches around the waistline. He barked, rather than talked, at his subordinates.

Since his fleet was pretty much in tatters as the result of their battles with barbarian raiders, Mendez moved his headquarters to Pizar, the single planet revolving around Proxima Centauri, where the best shipyards in the system were located. There he laid down the keels of forty battle wagons of latest design.

He equipped the ships with radiation cannon which could trigger atomic fusion in targets a thousand miles distant. He equipped each gun with the equivalent of an old time proximity fuse so that its beam, which could not be aimed accurately at such a range, would automatically seek out, center on and disintegrate any moving object larger than a meteor. (He had to put that limitation on to avoid draining his power packs on the hunks of rock which floated endlessly through deep space.)

While this work was in progress, the admiral's P.R.O.'s used their persuasive powers to such good effect that they enlisted thousands of the husbands, brothers and sons of the kidnapped women of Pizar. Women were scarce on that drab planet and their relatives swore they would put up a real fight to get them back. Finally, the recruits were put through an intensive course of hypnotic sprouts to train them for the exacting work of manning the new fleet.

All this took time, of course, but Mendez was not molested. It was reported that the barbarians still were licking the wounds administered to them by Merek.

That upstart, incidentally, made Mendez's life miserable with suggestions which were, as any admiral and Second Gen could see, completely impractical. To make things worse, the youth—he wasn't over fifty if he were a day—had to live within his meager captain's pay because he had never made a deposit, and therefore received no dividends from the Bank. He wore readymade uniforms; he had a shock of sandy hair which no issue pomade could conquer. He had big feet which banged the furniture. He had big hands which, Mendez did not know, were sensitive as a girl's when plotting a chart or nursing a vernier. Moreover, he actually read the ancient textbooks on strategy and tactics and had a fixation that guerrilla warfare was not outmoded.

"Great spacetime, Captain!" the admiral would bark like an Airedale when his nerves wore thin. "Think in terms of parsecs, not paratroops; of astrogation instead of assassination." He longed to break the fool but, in view of Marian's remarks, he would have to wait for a real slip before doing so.

"Yes sir. Sorry sir," was the captain's reply to every rebuke. Then he would salute as smartly as his tight uniform would let him, wedge himself through the door and go back to his quarters on the light cruiser assigned to him. There he would study and re-study accounts of guerrilla battles, from those of the ancient Tartars to that absolutely impossible barbarian raid on Pizarport.

"I still can't understand it," he said one night to Lieutenant Pancrief, as they sat in semi-isolation nursing beers in the Pizarro Cafe. "The barbarians sneaked their big clumsy ships through to Pizar without making a pip on a single radar. They crashed the ball, which means that they knew how to dress, act and talk exactly as we do, although we have been led to believe they are a bunch of stinking morons. When we attacked they retreated in perfect order."

"Um," said Pancrief, "they were scared to stand and fight."

"I'm not so sure. They wanted those women...alive."

"They sure pulled a disappearing act," the lieutenant admitted. "One minute we were knocking out their ships like sitting ducks. The next minute, Poof!"

"Well, how in spacetime did they do it? That's what I want to know."

"I always figured they went into overdrive." Pancrief signaled for more beer.

"Nonsense. It takes hours to warp into hyperspace. An instantaneous warp would have killed everyone aboard the barb ships."

"Maybe it did." The lieutenant blew away the foam which filled half his glass. "We haven't heard a peep out of them since."

"I don't believe that either. It was some sort of guerrilla trick like one I read about where scouts disguised themselves as dead trees. Their enemies were looking for live men, so the scouts became 'invisible.'"

"Could be. Rolph the Red is smart, even if he is a barb. Went to school on Mercon, didn't he?" Pancrief munched at a fistful of pretzels.

"Yes, that was when he was crown prince and we were friends with his father, Rolph the Golden. The prince took a twenty-year college course in four years."

"Nuts. More than a year of unbroken hypnosis will kill anybody."

"Didn't kill young Rolph. He went home, seized the throne and started moving in on us."

"That's gratitude for you. Kick us in the teeth after we befriend 'em. This time, though, we'll knock his dirty teeth out."

"Don't quote me," said Merek, "but I'm not so sure of that." He picked up the check and rose to his feet, knocking over his chair as usual.

They left the cafe and plodded through the frost-rimed city.

"You know," said the lieutenant as they stopped to light cigarettes under a street lamp. "I can't understand what we've got that the barbs want. All that out there," he waved a long arm toward the stars, "and they start crowding us."

"There's something beyond the fringe of the galaxy they're afraid of."

"Afraid? Those babies will spit in the eye of a twark."

"Yes, because they know how to fight—and tame—a twark. But they're just grownup children. They're superstitiously afraid of the…the unknowable, Rolph once called it."

"You went to school with him, Merek?"

"Well, not exactly *with* him. He…existed in my dorm. We used to talk a bit when the hypnos let him up long enough to fill him full of food. I gather things are pretty rugged out on the Omega Centauri star cluster where he hangs out. Even in those days Rolph talked about moving his people back into the galactic plane—back to Earth, even, until I explained that that was impossible."

"Why don't the barbs ask us to join forces with them against the Whaty-oumaycallit?"

"Rolph did, I gathered. He made quite a play for Marian at one time, until she told him Mercon's fighting days were over."

Pancrief ground out his cigarette butt in the light snow underfoot and followed his superior up the ramp to the deck of their shining, cigar-shaped cruiser.

CHAPTER V

One year after his arrival on Pizar, Admiral Mendez lifted his new fleet for its long flight out of the plane of the galaxy toward the lonely Omega star cluster. There had been ceremonies first, of course—ceremonies replete with gold braid and golden words. The pale Pizarians listened politely as they stood in the wan light of Proxima, their impassive faces cross-hatched by the slanting beams of distant Alpha and her twin.

They applauded Mendez's clichés as he told them that the best defense was an offense and that the sanctity of the home must be preserved. Under the eyes of their Merconian and Arconian officers, the new Pizarian crew members tossed their white caps into the cold air and cheered lackadaisically.

Finally it was over. The natives went about their mysterious affairs. Mendez barked at his staff officers. Tritium rockets spluttered as they warmed. Ports screwed shut. When the two score stately ships blasted out of their cradles and arrowed toward their "rendezvous with destiny" the spaceport was almost deserted.

"My people are not demonstrative," Pancrief said, as he stood with Merek on the bridge of the cruiser *Meadowlark*. They had little to do but stand; the autopilot had taken over and was nursing the ship upward at a steady 1G acceleration.

"Your people have never forgiven the First Council for ordering them to colonize rocky little Pizar and sending the main body of colonists on to the lush planets of Mercon and Arcon."

"It's a good life on Pizar," Pancrief defended. "We don't get rich. Our dividends can't compare with yours. Still…"

"Still, Pizar's Second Gens nurse a grudge."

"How can they nurse a grudge for a millennium? They've Banked all that."

"I remember reading about a civil war in the United States, Pan. The hatreds it engendered didn't die out for five generations. Isn't the same thing true on Pizar?"

"Well yes, maybe. They like to think they remember the good old days. Sometimes I believe they do, in a way. There is resentment."

"Let's hope it has been hypnoed out of the crews," said the captain. "To be on the safe side, I'll order daily drills and rigid inspections."

In perfect formation, the fleet went up and out of the gravitational grip of the three Centauran suns. A week after take-off they were sufficiently in the clear to start the slow and painful business of shifting into hyperspace.

At first the raw crews behaved quite decently as the stars winked out, green mist invaded the ships, and the muscular twitchings started. Each ship was on its own, for no communication was possible among them. Each captain used his own judgment as to the amount of pain his men could stand. Each, because of the sheer terror of hyperspace, tried to fight through as though demons pursued him.

Two sailors died, gibbering on the decks, the first "day" the *Meadowlark* spent in that never-never dimension. Six had bone-breaking convulsions the next day. The third was too much. Mutiny broke out in the engine room and ravened forward. But the twitching green ghosts who started it were in such agony and bewildered fright that Merek's officers managed to split them up, herd them to their quarters, and lock them in with a minimum of bloodshed.

After that the ship took care of herself as best she could with a few assists from sick and overworked officers. The crew's quarters were a shambles of writhing, screaming Pizarians. The ship's doctor and his apothecary's mates sweated it out around the clock. Merek and Pancrief toiled unceasingly over the unified field mathematics which alone could bring them out of hyperspace with a ship which did not resemble a flaming pretzel.

On the morning of the sixth day the captain stretched out a trembling claw and pushed home a sort of corkscrew which, he hoped, was the proper quadrant. A mewling caricature of a thing which had to be Pancrief, although it looked like Beelzebub, cut the warp.

Like a pip out of an orange, the *Meadowlark* snapped out of the green hell into a black space bounded by the orange on one side and a limitless, varicolored tapestry on the other. "Made it, once more!" Pancrief husked as he slumped in his chair and mopped his white face.

"Some didn't." Merek counted the silver ships floating in ragged disarray. "...thirty-four, thirty-five, thirty-six. One battle wagon, a cruiser and two destroyers left stuck in the warp."

"Poor devils." His aide staggered to his feet and leaned his forehead against the cold glass of the viewport. "Fringes of Omega Globular Star Cluster dead ahead, sir," he reported. "Alpha Centauri 20,000 light years astern. God pity the poor sailors who make a run like this."

Cutting in the transmitter, Merek made his report to the admiral.

"Ten men dead, you say?" barked a familiar voice from the flagship

Alpha. "Unfortunate. Very unfortunate." Then: "We blast for Rolph's headquarters planet at 2300. Here are your orders!" The mechanical voice of the fleet's main calculator cut in with a stream of gibberish which made sense only to the smaller "brain" in the *Meadowlark's* control center.

"Wish you could have asked the Old Man how many sailors *he* lost," growled Pancrief as his chief joined him at the port. "Lord, what a sight," he breathed after an interval. "One hundred thousand suns—count 'em— one hundred thousand. And packed thick as strawberries in a crate."

He stared at the flattened orange which was Omega Centauri. It glittered with numberless points of light, each one a giant star.

After that sight lost its appeal they moved to the opposite port to look back over the distances they had traversed in less than a week. The concentric rings of stars which made up their home galaxy stretched away, like some limitless dream tapestry. They were observing the Milky Way from "outside" now and so distant that the naked eye could not pick out any well-known starmark.

Between the star cluster on one side and the galaxy on the other there was nothing—nothing but an overwhelming blackness spangled at vast intervals by misty smears which represented immeasurably distant nebulae.

"Lonesome, isn't it?" Pancrief's usual bounce was missing.

There was a rap on the door. Lieutenant (J. G.) Manfred entered and saluted smartly, though his uniform was dirty and sweat-stained.

"Most of the crew have returned to normal, sir," he said.

"Pipe them to battle stations and give each a double ration of Scopio, Lieutenant," Merek replied. "We start moving in at 2300."

Manfred saluted again and departed, humming. He had been transferred from the flagship to the cruiser at Merek's request. The informal atmosphere on the *Meadowlark* made him feel as if rescued from a long stretch in prison.

The fleet reformed on schedule and arrowed toward the star cluster. Omega enlarged rapidly but nothing came up to meet the invaders.

"It's not like Rolph," said Merek as he puffed nervously at a cigarette a week later and studied the Cepheid variable star which now winked dead ahead, like a celestial lighthouse. "I can't believe we'll catch him napping."

"Maybe it's a trap," suggested Manfred, who was standing the watch with him.

"Space is too big to do much trapping in. I'm worried, though, that Rolph is out raiding us while we're raiding him."

"I doubt it, sir. Unless his espionage is weaker than we think, he knows we're coming by now. And he can't take a chance on losing his base of supplies."

"If he *has* a base in the accepted sense, Lieutenant. I have a hunch this war is something your modern textbooks never got around to discussing."

By the time the Cepheid had waxed and waned twice more in its endless, thirteen-hour cycle, they were within its planetary system and coming in for a landing on one of its two Earth-type worlds.

Radar screens up, guns swiveling in search of non-existent enemies, the ships decelerated together like one mechanism. Early the next "morning," before the Cepheid sun was half way to its maximum brightness, they landed in circle formation on a snow-covered plain rimmed by grim mountains where a river cataracted a thousand feet into an ice-filled sea.

"Intelligence says this is the site of Rolph's capital," the admiral's puzzled voice came over the communicator. "Looks deserted, but keep a sharp lookout. I'm sending out scouts."

As a half dozen destroyers darted away, the crews of the grounded ships stood tensely at their posts. But nothing happened. Only the voices of operators aboard the scouts came over the radio. After an hour, Mendez called a staff meeting on the bluff overlooking the heaving ocean.

"There's been a slip-up," the admiral growled as he pulled his greatcoat around his ears against the chill wind. "This can't be the place."

"I'm not so sure, sir," Merek ventured. "Notice that crisscross of depressions in the snow. Streets would look that way after a blizzard."

"Streets! But there are no houses in sight."

Merek started kicking into the fresh drifts, which lay about two feet deep. Almost immediately his boot hit an obstruction. He cleared around it, disclosing a stake which had been driven slantwise into the ground.

"Tent peg," he explained. "The barbarians live in tent cities. They've decamped."

"Impossible, Captain," barked the admiral. "The barbs don't have enough ships to move an entire population. We've landed on the wrong planet, somehow."

A destroyer materialized in the leaden sky and flamed in for a landing. Out tumbled a captain who herded two captives before him. One was a powerful, middle-aged man with one arm, the other was, very evidently, a woman. Despite the fact that the thermometer was still below freezing, their only clothing consisted of boots, gloves and fur kilts which covered them from navel to mid-thigh. Both wore their hair in braids and the man had a long reddish-grey beard.

"Are you subjects of Rolph the Red?" Mendez bellowed when the strange pair stood before him, erect and contemptuous. He acted on the assumption that any foreigner could understand English if it were shouted loud enough.

"Nah!" sneered the man.

"Who are you then?"

"Rolph brudder, sister."

"What?" Mendez goggled, thinking he had made a haul indeed.

"Aw, barb brudder," the fellow enlightened him.

"Brothers, eh?" The admiral covered his chagrin with a frosty smile. "Where, then, are Rolph and his *fighting* men?"

The barbarian took no offense. He stared down at the stump of his arm for a moment, then broke into a slow, knowing smile. "Mind Pizar?" he asked. "Brian," he tapped his hairy chest, "fight dere. Lose arm. Fin' mudder." With his good arm he gave the woman an affectionate whack.

The admiral stepped back as if struck. "You? A Pizarian?"

"Not any more," the woman answered coolly. "Fact is, I have almost forgotten Pizar. Dreadfully dull hole, isn't it, Admiral Mendez?"

"You'll return home with the fleet, of course."

"No thank you. Not unless you put me in irons."

"You like it here—this miserable, godforsaken iceberg…this lout?"

"I adore it."

"How do you keep from freezing, running around half naked?" Mendez demanded.

"How do you keep from suffocating inside that uniform?"

"Enough of your insolence," yelled the outraged admiral. "Where is Rolph?"

"Up there." She pointed to a spot of light in the sky which marked the Cepheid's second planet. "He pulled up stakes here when he heard you were coming. I understand he has arranged a hot reception for you on Midgard. Have fun."

"You treasonable hussy! Get out of my sight before I *do* put you in irons."

The ex-Pizarian dropped him a curtsy, linked her arm with that of her mate and trudged off across the snow without a backward glance.

"Well." For once Mendez was almost speechless. "We re-embark at once. Attack formation."

CHAPTER VI

Their cautious flight to Midgard took a full week. Their reward was a parched desert. Scouts reported sighting only a few thousand barbarians.

"Decamped again, the flea-bitten coward," raged Mendez at another futile staff meeting, "though how he does it I cannot understand. The only thing to do is to garrison these planets and hunt him down in space."

"Perhaps the emperor has gone to the planetary system of some neighboring star," suggested Rear Admiral Pierce. (He would have ranked as a full admiral, except for the unfortunate fact that he had been born on Pizar.) "I understand the barbarians control five or six of them."

"We'll cross that bridge when we come to it."

"Do you think it advisable to divide the fleet, sir?" Merek ventured.

"Dismissed!" was the admiral's only reply.

Five cruisers were placed temporarily under Merek's command and sent back to their first landing place while another five were left with Pierce at Midgard. A month later the rest of the fleet was caught off-guard in what should have been the empty space between two stars.

When disjointed, panic-stricken reports of the battle started dribbling in, Merek and Pierce raced out to give what help they could. All they found was the *Alpha*, which the barbarians had pointedly ignored. The rest of the ships were only shining notes of cosmic dust.

"I don't understand. I don't understand," Mendez babbled after the remnant of the fleet had made good its escape via hyperspace and was limping homeward through the fringe or the galaxy. "One minute our detectors were quiet as the grave. The next, those barb ships were amongst us, so close we couldn't bring our guns to bear without hitting each other. They cut us to ribbons. But the crowning insult was they never fired a shot at the *Alpha*. Not a shot, sirs. Not a shot." He buried his stricken face in his hands.

"It was treachery," shouted Marlborough, captain of the flagship. "It was the Pizarians among us. I never trusted the…"

"I resent that," snarled Pierce. He thrust out a stubbly jaw and seemed about to leap at the other, across the empty table.

"There were no Pizarians on the detectors," Mendez said. "I had seen to it that they couldn't be in a position to…"

"I resent that even more," yelled Pierce. "My countrymen are loyal. And they're fighters—not like you effete Merconians."

"Gentlemen," Merek cut in, "this is no time for bickering. The system's in grave danger."

"The boy's right," said Mendez and then, to show he bore no grudge: "What is your explanation of our, uh, setback, Captain Merek?"

"The barbs came at you out of hyperspace, sir."

"That's impossible. Instantaneous transit would have killed every man aboard their ships."

"How do you know there *were* men aboard? Perhaps they've made common cause with some alien race."

"Those bloody Siriuns," brooded the admiral. "Well," he took a grip on himself, "what's left of the fleet must proceed immediately to Pizar for refitting. I'll take the *Alpha* on to Mercon and," he fished forlornly for the proper slang term, "and get my needin's."

* * * *

This time Marian did not extend either hand to be kissed. "A year and a half wasted, Mendez," she purred. "A billion dollars wasted. Thirty-eight hundred Merconian lives wasted. You have six months left."

"Six months! Your Intelligence wouldn't hold me to that?"

"I would." Her slender, gold-tipped fingers played with a spool of recording tape he had brought—tape which portrayed the fleet's debacle.

"But the morale of my men is shot."

"More slang, Mendez, or do you mean that literally?"

"Destroyed," he amended. "It will take me months to get them in fighting trim again and train new recruits."

"Recruits?" Those sapphire eyes narrowed. "No one will join, the fleet while the memory of our defeat is green."

"Conscript them, then, confound it."

"Conscription would have to be approved by the people. This is a democracy."

"Then have the Council try to make some sort of compromise with Rolph. He's in trouble out on Omega. Perhaps, if we…invited him to come…"

"Compromise!" She forgot her studied calm. "No! Centauran blood must never be diluted. We are a super race. Better extinction than that!"

"There was a time when you thought otherwise," he said softly.

"Oh!" Her face flamed. "You are referring to that gossip about Rolph and me. Be careful, Mendez. You may presume too far."

"There might be another way," he floundered. "That last batch of refugees from Earth—the ones who came here about a century ago—think like barbarians in many ways. Perhaps, if we asked their advice…"

"Mendez. Mendez," she sighed. "Is this the best you have to offer? The refugees are unalterably opposed to war of any kind. Their ancestors saw it destroy Earth. They would tell us to practice passive resistance… And *I* still say you have six months more, Mendez. If there is no victory by that time, Rear Admiral Merek will assume command of the fleet."

"Rear Ad…" He tore at his collar. "There may be another line of attack."

"Yes?" There was a hint of feline merriment in the word.

"Have the Council change the law regarding Bank deposits. Surely it has the power to do *that* without a referendum. Command all citizens of the Three Planets to deposit all recollections of the past month."

"Go on!" She leaned forward with that liquid motion which set his pulses hammering.

"With memory of the Omega disaster wiped out, I can easily recruit more men. Then, when additional ships now being built on Pizar are completed, the fleet will rise like…who was that giant whose strength was renewed every time he was thrown to the ground?"

"Antaeus," she answered promptly. "But, as I remember it, Hercules finally defeated the giant by strangling him in mid-air. Nevertheless, your idea is a good one. The people murmur. Pizar is in almost open revolt. They will quiet down when their minds are washed clean of the defeat."

"Thank God," husked Mendez. "Now I will be able to sleep again."

Marian threw back her fine head and laughed until the calculator panels tinkled. "You! The order which the Council issues will not apply to you, to Council members, or to Merek. We must have some continuity."

"But I could *read* about my defeat, or study it on the screen. I wouldn't have to see those fine ships puffing into nothingness every time I close my eyes. And I wouldn't see that 'I told you so' look on Captain Merek's face."

"Rear Admiral Merek," she corrected. "And don't forget. Six months!"

He stomped out of the room without waiting to be dismissed.

In her library, Marian fitted the film she had been toying with onto a spindle, found a spot which showed Merek on the bridge of the *Meadow-lark* and enlarged the three-dimensional image until it filled one end of the room.

* * * *

There were plenty of complications, but no real hitches, when the Order in Council was promulgated. For several weeks the thousands of branch Banks in communities on Mercon, Arcon and Pizar were open around the clock as their operatives processed some two billion Centaurans. Depositors dutifully wrote memos to themselves about the most important activities in which they were engaged. Then they sat in quiet little booths with electrodes clamped to their temples while all knowledge of recent events was transferred from the "punched molecules" of their brain cells to almost identical molecules and circulating memory columns of the fantastic cybernetic calculator—or rather the endless series of calculators—which constituted the Memory Bank. They left their booths suffering from a species of induced amnesia, were presented with the memos they had written, read them—and carried on.

No attempt was made, or could be made, to completely wipe out mention of the Omega debacle in printed or photographed news records. But records are ghostly substitutes for actual memories, since they have comparatively little emotional impact; few people bother to re-read them, once they are outdated.

So the Centaurans awoke, as from a nightmare which they could no longer recall. Again there was polite chatter along the green avenues, and laughter in the spacious homes and vaulting theaters. Oh yes, they realized vaguely that there had been a battle of some kind and that the barbarians were still a threat. But meantime the sun shone, the larks sang and an endless, placid and almost effortless life was to be lived and cherished.

Even on restless Pizar, Mendez was treated with polite respect.

"Makes you feel a bit sick, doesn't it?" said Merek to Pancrief. The latter, a captain now, and elevated to command of the *Meadowlark*, was supervising the work of grinding hyperspace burn off the ship's sleek hide. "We have the tar whaled out of us. We learn some valuable lessons as a result. Then, *presto chango*, the Council waves a wand and we're right back where we started. Instead of including seasoned veterans, the new crews will be made up entirely of raw recruits."

"I wouldn't know, sir. I've had my amputation, too. Every once in a while it's like going down a stairway with an occasional tread missing, or like using bifocal glasses for the first time. Ugh!"

"I'm sorry, Pan," said Merek later, as they sat amidst the top brass, but still not of it, at the slowly turning bar of the Pizarro. "I tried my best to get you and the other officers exempted but the Old Man wouldn't hear of it."

"Hates you, doesn't he?"

"Can't say I blame him, with the Council pushing me ahead this way. I wonder why. Most officers don't rate lieutenant commander until they've made at least one regular deposit."

"Two reasons," grinned his friend. "In the first place, you have real ability."

"And the second reason?"

"You'll find that one in your mirror!... Of course, these emergency deposits may be a good thing, at that. Everyone seems full of bounce. I feel that way too, most times,... And then, in the middle of the night I wake up and get to thinking that things must be terribly bad to make the Council resort to such a thing as has been done to us."

"I've told you…"

"I know you've told me. And I've studied the recordings. But I'm still not convinced. Maybe I just can't trust anybody who cuts a hunk out of my life."

"I see." Merek bit his lips. "But it isn't a permanent loss, like a regular deposit. You'll get your memories back after the war ends."

"Maybe, *if* the war ends soon. And maybe, if it doesn't, I'll be making more deposits. Say, do you think the Second Gens feel, all the time, the way I do now…? Feel they've lost something precious forever? Is that why the Old Man hates us Non-depositors? Is that why he only feels at home with fogs?"

"Fogs?"

"Yeah. F-o-g-s. Fine Old Gentlemen of the Second Generation, like those he's talking to over there now."

"You're talking too much," said Merek. "Let's be getting back to the Yard."

* * * *

This time Admiral Mendez had only twenty-one ships at his back when he made a second ringing farewell speech to the Pizarians. Still, it was a formidable array, far stronger than Intelligence guessed the barbarians could put into space.

There was the fifteen-hundred foot *Alpha*, complete with a new set of teeth. There were ten new battleships, their turrets modified so they could fire point blank at short range with no danger of radiation backlash. Five of these, including his own ship, the *Centaur*, had been placed under Merek's command. The other battle wagons were under Marlborough. The cruisers and destroyers which had escaped from Omega also had been hastily modified to make them more deadly. An Arconian named Anderson commanded the cruiser flotilla and a Pizarian old timer, Pratt, had been called in to handle the destroyers. (Fiery little Pierce was relegated to a desk job in the Navy Yard.)

So they went out.

So they negotiated hyperspace.

So, as they lay waiting for orders to reform and advance on the star cluster, they were swept by what seemed to be a harmless cloud of small meteors.

And hell popped! Within five minutes of the appearance of the meteors, ship after ship caught fire! Their hulls blazed with scores of points of light. Their radio voices emitted startled squawks of astonishment and alarm.

"Marlborough! Merek! Anderson! Pratt!" The admiral stuck strictly to protocol in calling the roll. "Report!"

"We have struck a barbarian mine field, I think," gobbled Marlborough.

"We've been boarded," said Merek.

"Boarded? In deep space? You're crazy!" raged Mendez.

"Yes sir. Over."

"Hull punctured in four places," cut in an hysterical voice hardly recognizable as that of the usually phlegmatic Anderson. "Losing air rapidly. Getting crew into space suits. All other cruisers in trouble."

"Same here," came Pratt's muted voice. "Hull melting dozens places. No time for suits. Goodbye, sir."

A spot of crimson appeared on the wall of the bridge not five feet from where Merek stood. It spread like a boil. The titanium metal began to bulge outward ever so slightly. The *Centaur* was being hulled.

"Mendez. Give me the air," Merek shouted over the babble which filled the ether. "I'm going to try a maneuver which may save us. No time to explain. If it works, follow my example... Pancrief. Come in!"

"Yes sir!" The *Meadowlark* lay only a few miles from the *Centaur* but its captain's voice was muffled and faint, showing he had already donned a suit.

"Roll your ship. I'm going to scratch your back. Do the same for mine if you can." He left the switch open as he shouted directions. Slowly the *Centaur* began to roll on her axis. As she did so, her guns trained on the *Meadowlark*, which also had started to roll, like a flaming pinwheel.

"Barely tap the firing keys!" Merek commanded his gunners. "Two bursts. Sear both her sides. Ready, Pan? Follow suit. Hold tight, everyone. Fire!"

Simultaneously, lances of purple radiation flashed from both ships.

Merek was slammed to port as by a giant hand, missing the deadly red spot by only a foot. Manfred, who had been at the controls, was catapulted from his chair to pile on top of his superior. The big ship bucked like a bronco, although only a whiff of radiation had touched it.

The spot began to fade and reports from other parts of the *Centaur* said similar port side blisters were doing likewise. But, as Merek and Manfred dragged themselves back to their posts, a crimson smudge grew on the starboard wall of the bridge.

Merek saw that the *Meadowlark* also had been slammed back on her haunches. Half of her was scorched and black from his fire. But the part of her hull presented as she continued to roll still sparkled with a dozen pinpoints of vicious brilliance.

"Fire!" Merek ordered as both ships presented their burning flanks as targets. This time he gripped a control panel and braced himself. His fingernails splintered, his feet shot out from under him and he smashed against the wall alongside Manfred. This time the pilot did not rise.

"Pan? You all right?" The teetering hulk outside was all black now and remained visible only because it occluded a part of the galaxy.

"O.K. What's left of us," came the rejoinder. "*Centaur* sure carries a wallop. I have a broken shoulder, I think. I've got the boys patching and strengthening the hull. What hit us?"

"Tell you later." Merek scanned the heavens and added: "Most of the ships got the idea and are cleansing each other. But a lot of them, including the *Alpha* are still burning and out of control. Can you help me spray the flagship?"

"Yes sir."

Merek staggered to the pilot's seat and put the ship about. As he passed the twinkling *Alpha* to port his gunners gave her the one-two. The *Meadowlark* seared her from the opposite quarter.

"Admiral Mendez!" he called when the maneuver was completed.

There was no answer, although he thought he heard an agonized gasp. "Marlborough?"

"No air," came the dazed reply. "Half of crew suffocated. Patching."

Matter-of-factly, now that the emergency had passed, Anderson made a somewhat similar report. Pratt did not answer.

As Merek kept probing he found that ten ships in all showed signs of life. Eventually, Captain Merryman of the *Alpha* managed to crawl to the mike and report Mendez with a fractured skull and a third of the flagship's crew either suffocated or incapacitated from injuries received when she had been seared.

"I propose Merek should take command," said Anderson after the sad roll call ended. "None of us would be alive except for him. What do you say, Marlborough?"

"At your command, Admiral Merek," came the answer.

"None of the reporting ships are badly damaged, but only thirteen have replied," said the new admiral. "I have a hunch the barbarian fleet will be here in full force very shortly. If we try to put crews aboard the death ships, we'll have no time to get back into hyper. On the other hand, we can't allow those ships to fall into enemy hands. We've got to beam them down. I'll do the dirty work. The rest of you get shipshape. Any objections?"

There were none. After one last call to the drifting ships, many of which still burned fiercely, the *Centaur's* guns spoke again and again. At each broadside a splendid hulk, perhaps with injured men still aboard, flamed into dust.

When it was all over, Merek leaned his head against the control board and wept.

Then came the job of shepherding his undermanned cripples back into the relative safety or hyperspace. Technicians had to be shifted from ship to ship to make the maneuver possible. Time flew while Merek searched the heavens.

The last straw came when, after all the other vessels had melted through the barrier, Pancrief reported the *Meadowlark's* warper damaged beyond repair by the jolts it had received. Then there were more frantic orders and shuttling of lifeboats. At last Merek himself regretfully pressed the trigger which sent his first command to join her dead sisters.

"Thanks for that final blast," a new voice boomed through the *Centaur's* loudspeaker. "Gave us a chance to get a dead fix on you. You're bracketed. Will you surrender?"

"Go to hell, whoever you are!" Merek did not feel as brave as he sounded. The radar screen showed points of light converging on the *Centaur* from all points.

"Emperor Rolph the Red of Barbarie here."

"Admiral Merek of Centaurus here. My comment still stands."

"I thought you wouldn't give up the ship. All right then. Get your men—and yourself—into the boats and blow her. I'll pick you up. Fair enough?"

Merek hesitated. Tradition said to die fighting. He looked at Pancrief.

"You're a long time dead," said that worthy, who stood beside him on the bridge nursing his bandaged shoulder. "Live to fight another day. While there's life, there's hope. Dead men tell no tales."

"Oh, shut up!... Rolph, will you give us an hour to abandon ship?"

"Of course. But don't try a dash for hyper. We'll nail you."

An hour later and a score of miles away, the *Centaur's* lifeboats, with 500 men aboard, bobbed like corks as their ship's pile went up in a final blaze.

CHAPTER VII

"It looks like a chunk of honeycomb," marveled Pancrief as the boat in which he, Merek, and half a hundred badly battered sailors were jammed edged toward an open pressure hatch of the barbarian flagship. (The others already had been picked up by one or another of twenty enemy vessels.)

"Or the faceted eye of some monster insect," Merek agreed.

"Stuck together with spit, too," added Pancrief, as the ship loomed above them. "How they got that crazy hatch open without a blowtorch is beyond me."

The impression of disorderly order, if such a thing is conceivable was heightened as fur-kilted, grinning warriors of both sexes prodded the prisoners out of their boat and herded them down a long corridor to an accompaniment of skirling bagpipes. Segments of the floor were raggedly joined, sometimes with draughty cracks as much as a foot wide between the metal plates. Scratched and dented walls were pierced by portholes which seemed to have no possible use. The ramshackle structure creaked and groaned continuously, like a sailing ship at sea.

"And to think that the best Centaurus had was licked to a frazzle by near-brutes riding pieces of junk like this," groaned Pancrief, whose wound was bothering him badly. "To make it worse, half of these savages are girls!"

"Um!" Merek was trying to adjust himself to the fact that there seemed to be absolute equality between the barbarian sexes. "And I didn't see any guns mounted on this ship."

"Only ones I noticed were on a few Centauran merchantmen which Rolph probably bought while he was on Mercon and converted afterward."

"If only we could have had just one crack at these egg crates," sighed Merek.

"Wish I had a shot of Scopio," said the Pizarian with a shiver. "This corridor is almost as cold as space. How do they stand it, prancing around in fur panties?"

A tall girl wearing a trim gray kilt and a steel helmet with incongruous floppy fur "ears" set rakishly on a tousle of black curls, stopped the procession at a dimly-lighted corridor intersection. "Oo Merek?" she demanded.

A burly captain jerked his thumb at the Merconian.

The newcomer looked him up and down with dawning recognition in her laughing eyes. She took in his torn uniform, the cut over his eye, and the nasty bruise on his cheek. Then she winked at him broadly.

"Ow, Merek. Come talk Brudder Rolph." She snicked a knife out of her jewel-studded belt and prodded him not too ungently ahead of her.

"Ask the Emp to send us a doctor...and some hot toddy," Pancrief called after them. Merek was too flabbergasted to answer. He had caught sight of the long, faint scar which crossed the body of his guard from shoulder to hip.

The prisoner entered Rolph's quarters to find the emperor seated on a heap of furs, reading an old-fashioned paper book. He looked up and winked. (Of course, the Merconian remembered now, that was the barbarian greeting to friend or worthy foe.)

"Hello, Merek," he said, rising and extending his hand, Centauran fashion. "I'd like to say you are looking well, but I'm afraid I'd be lying. Sit down. Lie down if you wish. Iskra..." He turned to the girl. "Bri'g foo'. 'Ot drink. Iskra is one of my best warriors," he added as she departed briskly.

"Did that slip of a girl lead the raid on Pizar?" Merek was easing his aching bones to the floor.

"That steel spring of a girl did," chuckled his host. "You'll find out what I mean the first time you try to cross her. She's going to be your warden."

"You *are* looking well, Rolph." Merek studied the bronzed giant. "Quite a bit older, though," some imp made him add.

"Yes, I'm pushing forty," Rolph answered, stroking his full red beard. "That's almost ancient for Omega. Well, I have three strong sons and a daughter, any one of whom could take my place."

Iskra returned with a golden platter heaped with dripping hunks of roast meat and with three silver-inlaid horns filled with a steaming liquid.

"You'll have to use your fingers," said the barbarian. "There's not a fork on board. As for a napkin..." He stepped to the wall, which was draped with priceless Pizarian silks, ripped off a square of the material and presented it with a flourish. "I'll try to do better by you when we get to Asgard... Skoal!"

"Asgard!" Merek choked over his drink. "Is that what you call your capital?"

"Why not?" For the first time Rolph seemed nettled. "Good old Terrestrial name, isn't it? I found it in a book of Norse legends."

"Oh yes." Merek felt better as the hot liquor warmed his stomach. "Will you send some of this to my crew, Rolph? They need it rather badly, along with a doctor." As the emperor nodded he added, "I suppose you call this stuff mead, too?"

"How did you know?"

"I, too, am one of those freaks who reads the old books. But the real mead was a kind of beer. This must be a hundred proof."

"Oh well, if you want to get technical, bagpipes are of Celtic origin. But I like bagpipes. They make pleasant music to die to."

Rolph sat down, presented the platter to his guest and then dipped into the meat with both hands. The girl followed his example. As she munched, she studied Merek quizzically. He returned the compliment; she was really something to look at with her creamy skin, turned-up nose and hair so black it seemed blue.

"Did you revive the old Norse mumbo-jumbo recently?" he asked when Iskra's calm scrutiny became embarrassing.

"No. My great granddaddy, Rolph the First, started it. I carried on."

"Why, for Pete's sake?"

"Because I, Rolph the First, studied philosophy," the emperor said between bites.

"*You*, Rolph the First? He has been dead a hundred years."

"I am his avatar, naturally."

"You believe in reincarnation?"

"My people believed in it after I explained it to them. Reincarnation makes them feel superior to you superior Centaurans. *You* get killed in a war or an accident and you're dead forever. If one of *us* dies today, he knows he will be reborn tomorrow. What chance have you got against us in the long run, if you must worry about saving your precious hides at every turn?"

"I see what you mean. But you were saying something about philosophy."

"Oh yes. I studied philosophy. I noticed that every people has a religion which perfectly fits its state of civilization. Until a hundred years or so ago my people out here on the fringe of nowhere had no religion—and no civilization to speak of either. You know our history. We were the last wave of pioneers to leave Earth for Alpha Centauri along the only route not blocked by alien races…and light years.

"You Centaurans had got away while the going was good, just before the first Terrestrial blowup in 1999. You had had 500 years to set up your tight little system before we arrived. Even then, you were too good to let our ragtag and bobtail move in with you. But you had developed an experimental form of hyperspace drive. You generously consented to let us make the first long-distance jump with it. Hah!" Rolph's white teeth flashed in a mirthless grin. "I've sung the old folksongs. I almost remember what happened. The first stop was Omega, a safe 20,000 light years away, you Centaurans thought. Ten percent of my people got through. Half of those died before they learned how to exist in a star cluster.

"Then, for almost 400 years we stagnated and retrogressed while we fought the cold, the twarks, the fees and each other. We went back about as far as men can go and still remain men. Cannibalism, you know. Human sacrifices. All that.

"About a hundred years ago you folks perfected the hyper drive and got through to us. A sorry lot you found us. I don't blame you for sending missionaries along with your merchant ships. Still, you were damned fools to do so."

"Why?" Despite his fascination with the story, Merek's eyelids were drooping.

"Because I—incarnated as Rolph the First then, you understand—decided it was time for my people to make their comeback. I—he—pumped your merchants and missionaries for information. He learned to read and write. He studied comparative religions and selected Norse mythology as the one best suited for his people's state of development. By the time he was, uh, translated in battle at the age of twenty-eight he had laid the groundwork for our present high state of civilization."

"High?" Merek was blinking sleepily at Iskra as she licked the grease of the feast off her fingers and wiped both hands on the fur of her kilt.

"It suits *us*," Rolph grinned as he followed the girl's example. "And it doesn't suit *you*. So it must be high. You don't understand us, of course. We're nomads—mechanized nomads, if you will. We hate cities. We hate conventions. We hate sham. We'd be perfectly content out here on Omega except for something which seems bent on herding us back toward Alpha… but I once told you about that."

"You mean what you called the unknowable."

"Yes." Rolph rose and began pacing the cabin, picking his teeth with the point of his sheathknife. "I tried to tell Marian that we faced a common danger. She wouldn't understand either… How is Marian, by the way?"

"Well," Merek answered the meaningless ritual. Centaurans were always well.

"A splendid woman. I thought of making her my empress for a time, but she's too bossy and set in her ways for life out here. Someday, someone may break through Marian's thousand-year-old shell of reserve and awaken the real woman in her again. Then you'll have something. In the meantime…" He ruffled Iskra's curls until she purred like a kitten. "…I'll put my bets on barbarian lassies like this one."

"Then if you could have made an alliance with Centaurus, you wouldn't be attacking us?"

"Of course not. We have nothing against you and you could teach us much. As it is, we're in the same position as the ancient barbarians who moved on lordly but decadent Rome, because the Tartars were pushing them from the rear."

"But how," mumbled Merek, dimly conscious that he was getting no information of real value, "how do you pull that disappearing act with your ships? And how did you set fire to our fleet?"

Rolph put his hands on his hips and roared with laughter.

"The first is a trade secret," he choked when he had recovered his breath. "As for the fires: that 'meteor swarm' was made up of barbarian commandoes wearing space suits and carrying atomic torches. They attached themselves to the hulls of your ships and drilled away until you blasted them."

"Yes, but," Merek's head was nodding despite his heroic efforts, "how did you know where we would emerge from hyperspace? 'S awful big."

"Unified field math, my boy. Knowing how you Centaurans hate to make the transit, I figured you'd take the shortest distance between two points in curved space. So I deployed a few thousand commandoes around the spot where you should have emerged—and you obliged. Now, as I was saying…"

But Merek wasn't listening. He had slumped sidewise on the be-furred couch and was dead to the world.

CHAPTER VIII

Merek awoke, stiff and sore. Wriggling experimentally, he found that he was stark naked and buried under a pile of furs which stank to heaven. He sat up, blinked in a semi-darkness split by a triangle of watery light, gasped as the cold bit him and huddled back among the covers.

"Hey there," he shouted.

A figure appeared in the triangle—it must be the open flap of a tent, he reasoned—advanced and bent over him.

"Hi, Merek," said Iskra with a wink.

"Hi yourself. I'm freezing. Where are my clothes?"

"Dere." She indicated a pile on the rush-covered floor, then appraised him blandly as, after a wait which produced no results, he scrambled into his uniform.

"Why was I stripped like that?" he asked to cover his embarrassment.

"Sleep warm nake'." She grinned. "Fur like skin."

"Um. I've read that the Eskimos thought that, too. Brrr! I'm freezing, even with my clothes on. How do you barb—how do you people stand it?"

"Barb aw face!" She slapped her bare chest proudly.

"I'll bet." He marveled at the unfrostbitten roundness of her tawny body. "There's more to keeping warm than that, isn't there now, Miss Iskra?"

"Miss? Name Iskra." Hearing his teeth chatter, she relented, dug into a pocket of her kilt and produced two dirty white pellets. "'Ere." She popped one into her mouth and offered him the other. "Eat. Get warm."

He followed her directions. Soon a generous warmth stole through his body. Some refinement of Benzedrine, he rationalized, amazed that the barbarians knew something about modern drugs. What a godsend for an army on the march! His body heat increased until it became almost uncomfortable. He removed his coat.

"Hung'?" asked the girl.

"Well, I most certainly could consume nourishment of some kind," he grinned.

"W'y use many word?" she puzzled, running her fingers through those crisp blue-black curls. "W'y no jus' say 'Yah'?"

"You must hail from Sparta," he chuckled as he followed her out of the round, leather-walled tent. "Wasn't it the Laconians who never used ten words when one would do?"

"Iskra no know. Good idee."

Merek dropped the argument to stare at the barbarian encampment. Round tents, made of some mottled, hairless skin, stretched in reasonably well-ordered rows along the brow of what was evidently the same bluff where Mendez's fleet had landed so long ago. Now the place was humming with activity. Before each of the endless hundreds of tents a group of barbarians squatted around a small stove of some sort, either cooking or eating breakfast. He noticed that each block of tents was surmounted by a tall pole from which fluttered the furry tails of animals. Looking more closely, he saw that every pole sported the tails of a different animal and that the kilts of the warriors were made from pelts of the fur for their tribal totem. On a hunch he pointed at Iskra's scanty garment and asked: "Rabbit?"

"Yah." She looked pleased. "Iskra belo'g Fightin' Rabbit Clan."

"Then you can't be much of a warrior," he couldn't resist teasing. "Rabbits don't fight where I come from."

"Omega rabbit fight, or die." She was frowning now. "Iskra show."

"Ouch!" Her slim fingers bit into his arm like a vise as she started leading him toward the nearest breakfasters, who also wore the gray fur.

They ate with twenty laconic warriors who, Merek surmised, made up Rolph's personal bodyguard. (The emperor's tent, larger than the rest and highly "decorated" with broken weapons, grinning skulls and other grisly trophies of battle, stood nearby, its back to the lonely sea.) Many of the guards bore their own battle trophies on their bodies. Even Iskra's beauty was marred by a scar.

When they had finished wolfing their meat and had washed it down with a drink called 'cof', which had not even a bowing acquaintance with coffee, Iskra dropped a bombshell. "Fool Merek say rabbit no fight," she announced. "Iskra now show." She picked two swords out of a nearby pile, tossed one toward the Centauran and made the other sing about her head.

"Now, look here," Merek protested, "Centaurans don't fight women."

"Better run fas', den," guffawed a one-eyed veteran who resembled pictures Merek had seen of the Norse god Odin.

"But I was only joking!"

Merek got his guard up just in time as the Amazon made a long spring at him, evidently in some ritual imitation of a rabbit's leap.

"Very well!" Cold anger surged up in him as her second cut almost parted his hair. "I'll teach you a lesson, even if I am stiff as a board. You're up against one of the best fencers on Mercon, young lady!"

Now fencing is an exact science. If Merek had been allowed to use his skill at it, he might soon have disarmed his lighter and shorter-reached opponent. The only trouble was that Iskra didn't fence. She came at him like the wild woman she was, using the edge of her sword instead of the point; slashing and chopping like a butcher at the block. Her guard was wide open, yet, when he thrust shrewdly, she was never there.

"Not let Iskra kill Merek, brudder," she husked at the guards, who had cleared a space for them in the snow. "Rolph say no."

Immediately she forgot her own orders and did her best to slice her opponent in two. As she fought, she began to lose, not only her beauty but her femininity and almost her resemblance to a human being. Her lips drew back from strong white teeth. Froth appeared at the corners of her mouth. Her slitted eyes gleamed red. Her curls turned wet and lank. Sweat bathed her body until it looked oiled and actually steamed in the cold wind. She became the unsexed steel spring of destruction which Rolph had hinted at.

Great star, thought Merek. *She's gone berserk.*

Merek fought well. He kept in the center of the yelling mob which now ringed the circle in the snow. He turned this way and that to meet her mad lunges.

Iskra was singing now, a chant which awoke a savage ancestral echo in some part of the Centauran's soul:

> *"Outta duh blackness,*
> *Into duh star shine,*
> *Fearless and daring,*
> *Come we, Rolph Brudder...*

The onlookers, who now included scores from nearby tent blocks, joined with her in roaring out the chorus:

> *"Forwar' to vict'ry!*
> *Kill aw Centauran!*
> *Steal dere fair women!*
> *Burn dere tall city!"*

The chant continued to unwind, but Merek had no time to listen; he was fighting for life. The heavy breakfast was slowing him down. So were the muscle strains of his recent battle. He kept to the defensive but before five endless minutes passed he was bleeding from a number of light cuts.

Iskra realized her advantage and bored in. Despite his best efforts, she drove him to the edge of the circle. The onlookers didn't budge and their jostling bodies interfered with his sword arm. The girl moved in for the kill.

"Stop!" Rubbing the sleep from his eyes, Rolph emerged from his tent. "Iskra! Rolph say stop!" He shouldered his way through the mob, hurling warriors right and left.

The berserker paid no heed. As Merek slipped on the treacherous footing and went to one knee, she swung her sword with both hands for a blow which would split his skull.

The emperor went through the ring like a mad bull. Just managing to grab her wrists, he twisted cruelly. The sword flew in one direction, Iskra in another. She lay gasping, all the air knocked out of her.

As the guards backed away from his deadly anger, Rolph sat down on a snow hummock, grabbed the girl by the scruff of the neck and turned her over his knee. Ripping off her jeweled belt, he applied it with a right good will where it would do the most good.

She tried to bite him. He tangled his fingers in her hair and continued the punishment. Gradually her struggles subsided, but not even a groan came through her clenched teeth.

At last the emperor rose, letting Iskra slide face downward into the snow. He doubled up her belt and tossed it toward his tent.

"Iskra through," he snarled. "Iskra be mudder now. Sew. 'Ave babe."

That brought a response, all right. She scrambled to her bare knees and wrapped her arms around her lord's legs. Her companions growled, but made no move. "Oh no," she pleaded. "Iskra goo' warrior…fi', ten year mo'. No make mudder. Please, Brudder Rolph!" Her face streaked with tears.

"Iskra no obey. Go berserk. Try kill. Rolph no trust."

"No. No. Jus' game. No kill." But she hung her head.

"Don't be too hard on her, Rolph," Merek interposed. "It's really my fault. I made fun of her totem. And she did tell the others not to let her kill me."

"I hate to lose her." The emperor chewed at his brick red moustache. "But I can't have warriors going berserk when not in battle. Don't want you killed, either, till they send your ransom, anyway. I'll get you another warden."

"Oh, she'll behave now. Besides, I want to learn how she uses a sword."

"If you say so, old friend." The red giant winked, then yanked the girl to her feet. "Iskra goo'?" he snarled. "Iskra obey?"

"Yah, Brudder Rolph." Despite heroic efforts she began to sniffle.

"Nex' ti'…" He crooked his neck, stuck out his tongue and gave a realistic imitation of a man on a gibbet. "Go get belt!" As she crept away, he added sweetly to the shuffling guards: "Fee 'ave big feast if Merek hurt!"

A wary intimacy grew up between Merek and his warden after their battle. She treated him as if he were made of delicate glass. She allowed him the freedom of the camp. And, from time to time, she let slip bits of information which he could never obtain from Rolph during his drinking bouts with the emperor.

At first he treated her like an overgrown child, on the theory that her primitive speech indicated an equally primitive mind. That was until he made an astounding discovery.

It came about in this ridiculous fashion: Water for baths was at a premium in camp. As a result, everybody itched. It was common courtesy, when seeing a neighbor suffering, to scratch his or her back. When Merek did this for Iskra or any of the other barbarians, they would frown and wriggle until he finally located the right spot. But, it gradually dawned, when they scratched *him*—or each other—they found the itch instantly and unerringly.

From this came the eventual realization that the barbarians employed some crude form of telepathy to express any but the simplest thoughts. That is, they used their few words to focus attention and then went on from there. They used words as sparkplugs which set off "explosions" of telepathic thought. And they showed justifiable annoyance when Merek insisted on babbling concepts at them which they had complete in their minds as soon as he had spoken three words.

Pancrief confirmed this theory when Merek visited Asgard's small, but surprisingly well-equipped tent hospital. "The nurse always shows up just before I get ready to call her. Psychologists have a theory that animals communicate in some such fashion but that men lost the art when they developed vocal speech. Probably telepathy had some sort of survival value in this godforsaken cluster and resulted in a mutation."

"But in that case, why is their vocal speech so horribly primitive?"

"I'm not so sure it is," came the surprising answer. "It's just stripped down to the running gears, like ancient Chinese. No grammar. No case endings. No pronouns. No tenses. And amazingly expressive. Maybe it's the language of the future, Merek." Pancrief sipped a horn of milk which stood at the bedside.

"But that would put the barbarians on a higher mental plane than us," Merek protested as he tried to plump up Pancrief's hard pillow.

"Never let Marian hear you say that. Besides, if you rate the barbarians above us just because they're somewhat telepathic, you'll have to put Siriuns up there too. They really do the job right."

"Ugh. Those slimy creatures. What a thought!"

"Think we'll get out of this?" Pancrief asked.

"If our ransom comes before Rolph starts moving in, so he can send us home under a flag of truce. If he takes us in the battleship, it may be different. I still doubt that he will be able to make a landing on Mercon."

"Providing he lands on Mercon," yawned Pancrief. "Did it ever occur to you that he may strike at Pizar, Arcon or even Beacon?"

"Pizar and Arcon are well protected. As for Beacon, it's only a chunk of barren rock. Nothing could live on it when it makes the transit between suns."

"Betcha these brutes could. And I'll also bet Rolph does have some more tricks. Have you seen his ships about, or any signs of a spaceport?"

"Come to think of it, no port big enough for battleships. When I asked Iskra about it, she just waved a hand at the sky."

"There you have it. I suspect he drugged the first meal we had after our capture, by the way. All of us slept three days. None of the fellows woke up in time to see us land, or to see what became of Rolph's ships."

Merek left the hospital in a thoughtful mood. And the evasive answers he received when he tried to question Iskra didn't help his state of mind. Try as he would, he could get no inkling of Rolph's plan of attack.

He got further when he worked up courage to ask the girl about the punishment with which Rolph had threatened her after their sword battle. (They fenced daily now, but the Amazon kept a tight rein on herself. About the only thing the contests did was to make Merek get into better physical condition than ever before.)

"On Omega ever'thi'g fight," she explained. "Twark fight. Fee fight. Man fight. Rabbit fight…or die quick."

"Yes," he fumbled, trying to put the question in such a way as not to offend, "but if the women fight, how do they find time to bear all the children I see scampering around?"

"Woman no fight. *Girl* fight."

"I don't get you."

"True long ti'," she struggled, blushing warmly. "Girl no 'ave babe till slow up…no goo' fo' fight."

"You mean mutation has made you a sort of female eunuch?" He recoiled.

"No!" Her eyes flashed. "Girl make love mebbe, yah. 'Ave babe, no!"

"I see." He wished he could read her thoughts the way she evidently read his. "And then, when a girl's reflexes start slowing down around thirty or so, she gets married and has a family. Right?"

"Married? Family?" Suddenly she seemed to understand. "Yah. Like so." She pointed to a buxom wench who was trudging through the tent rows, a baby strapped to her back, papoose-fashion and three older children tagging at her heels.

"But don't girls miss the excitement after they settle down?"

"No mo' girl. Woman," she corrected. "'Appy make 'ome wit' man… Tame fee. Watch twark. Build cell. Ver' busy. Ver' proud be mudder."

"What's a cell?"

Her black eyes, usually so direct, shifted evasively. "Merek want 'unt fee?"

"Sure. But first tell me what is a cell, and *then* what in blazes is a fee."

"Big fee 'unt tomorrow. Rolph say go. Merek feel stro'g now, no?"

"I feel strong now, yes," he gave it up. "When do we start?"

"Firs' 'our."

He calculated. The planet Asgard presented one face to its Cepheid sun at all times. During the five hours when that sun threw its minimum light— only about a twentieth as much as when at apogee—temperatures dropped below zero and became too cold for even the barbarians to be about much. That was when they retreated into their thick tents to carouse or sleep…and they seemed to require very little sleep.

The First Hour really came three hours after the Cepheid had hit its minimum brilliance and was building up for another "day." At that time the temperature rose above zero and the nightly snowstorm ceased.

From then on the camp was a beehive of activity for the eight half-way comfortable hours. By the Fourth Hour the snow was all gone, the sparse vegetation was growing madly and the old-fashioned Fahrenheit thermometers stood around sixty degrees under a sun which blazed with white, scorching heat.

As the next four hours passed, the temperature dropped slowly back toward zero. By the Ninth Hour both animals and vegetables had retreated into caves, tents or under the ground to withstand the frost and the blizzards.

* * * *

The dim sun was casting blood red shadows on the snowdrifts the next morning when Merek forced himself to leave his warm furs. Even with the help of Iskra's drug and a portable atomic hotplate which was the tent's only heating facility, he could not keep his stomach muscles from contracting painfully as he dressed.

Outside, he found several hundred warriors assembled, beating their bare arms against their naked chests when not consuming beakers of 'cof' and endless platters of stew.

At some unheard command, they marched off to an open space just beyond the tent city. Squatting haphazard on the plain were what looked like dozens of metal packing cases of weird shape and varying size. Cheery electric lights blazed from their round windows and the doors which opened to admit squads of warriors. After they were loaded, each crate rose and flew westward.

Merek blinked around his strange conveyance after he, Iskra and eight other braves had wedged themselves into it. It was a box, nothing more, which obviously was ordinarily used as living quarters by the pilot, his sleepy-eyed "mudder" and three grubby children. There was a control panel near the forward window. In the rear was a mass of apparatus which made no sense to the Centauran. As nearly as he could make out, it looked like a disconnected part of some larger machine. A light began to dawn in his mind.

"Cell?" he asked his warden.

"Yah."

"And thousands of cells are joined together, somehow, to make up one of Rolph's round spaceships?"

"Merek smart," she winked, then peered out of a porthole as a sign that no more questions would be welcome.

With the wind screaming around its corners like a banshee, the cell sped across the ghostly countryside at a height of several hundred feet and a speed of something like two hundred miles an hour.

"Las' 'unt?" the bearded, one-eyed warrior who looked like Odin, asked.

"'Ope so," Iskra replied. "Ti' gitdn' short."

"*It* come back."

"It alway' come back." She spat on the dirty floor. "More bad each ti'."

One-eye shuddered, poured a stiff drink of mead into himself, sat down against a wall, spread out his long legs, and snored.

"What is *It*?" Merek wanted to know.

"No can tell Merek wit' word. Bad."

The pilot began swearing at the top of his lungs, interrupting their conversation. Merek gathered that they had run into a head wind. The crate bucked, wabbled and slowed down to a crawl.

"Get late," groaned Iskra. "Fee wake."

They landed at last in wild hilly country. Other cells followed them in to form a circle several miles in diameter. The warriors took weapons from a rack and sallied out. The light was much stronger already and the temperature just below freezing.

"Stay wit' warrior," the girl told her prisoner. "Keep low. Shoot w'en Iskra shoot."

The ten spread out and began creeping toward the center of the circle. No orders were given. A prickling along his spine told Merek the barbarians had established a rapport and were working as a unit. "Odin" inched ahead of the rest, some sort of grenade in hand, toward a cave in the rocks.

"What...?" the Centauran began.

Iskra clapped a hand over his mouth.

"Twark nes'. Fee live dere too," she whispered in his ear. "Suck blood you'g, sick twark. Go 'way w'en sun warm. Mus' catch now."

Odin hurled his bomb into the cave. There was a muffled explosion. Bellowings and stampings within shook the ground. A triangular head, larger than that of an elephant and cloven with a triple row of yellow teeth, appeared for an instant at the opening. Merek's finger tightened on the trigger.

"No! Twark goo'!" Iskra grabbed his arm. "Wait."

A creature so monstrous that the very sight of it made the Centauran quail, crawled out of the cave. It had a head like a prehistoric saber-toothed tiger, except that a dozen backward-turning fangs instead of two protruded from its jaw. Behind these, and hanging below them, vibrated a mass of palps and mandibles. It had a hard, bulbous, laterally compressed yellow body covered with sparse long hairs.

The creature gathered its six abnormally long hairy legs under it and tried to make its escape. It did manage to bound six feet into the air, but it had been so badly gassed that, when it landed a good twenty feet from the cave mouth, it fell on its back and lay waving those awful legs in the air while its mandibles champed and slavered.

Ten guns spoke in unison. Merek expected the horror to be tom to bits by explosive bullets, but it seemed unharmed, although all movement ceased.

Another and another nightmare—a baker's dozen of them—scrambled out of the hole to be paralyzed by barbarian fire. When no more emerged the attackers ran forward and bound the legs of the fees with leather thongs. Merek lost his breakfast while engaged in the task.

In the next two hours they found and attacked four more caves and raised their bag to about three dozen. By this time the sun had grown quite bright and the temperature was well above freezing. So it was, that when they approached their sixth hole in the cliffs, out popped a dozen of the creatures before a bomb could be thrown. These made no move to escape but hurled themselves at the humans in fantastic, twenty-foot leaps.

"We warm bloo'. Fee like," Iskra explained cheerfully before she dived behind a rock and pumped her gun empty at the things.

The paralysis charges slowed up the attack but could not quite stop it. If each fee had picked a different enemy, the barbarians would have been in a bad way indeed. Instead, they converged on "Odin," who had been just a little slow in taking cover. They swarmed over the screaming man, slashing with their palps and sucking at his blood with a sound like pigs in a trough.

That gave the other warriors a chance to concentrate their fire. The paralysis pellets finally accomplished their work. The fees stopped their feeding, rolled over, kicked their legs a few times and were still.

"One-eye too ol', slow." Iskra looked at the bloodless husk of "Odin" after she and Merek had finished helping the others bind the fees.

"Aren't you sorry he was killed?" Merek was appalled.

"Why?" She was genuinely puzzled. "One-eye born 'gain soon. Grow stro'g. 'Ave two eye. Be warrior, few year."

"Don't you folks have any sort of Valhalla, where warriors killed in battle go to enjoy wine, women and song for a while?"

"Valhall'?" She looked at him with a trace of pity. "Valhall' barb name for Mercon."

"You're damned sure of yourselves, aren't you?" His face flushed.

She shrugged and joined her companions in piling a cairn of stones over the dead man. The day was now too warm to risk disturbing any more fees. They dragged their inert captives to a central spot and lounged in the sun until cells dropped out of the sky to pick them up.

CHAPTER IX

There was a combined hunt supper and wake at Asgard that night. (Several hundred fees had been captured—for what purpose Merek could not conceive—and six barbarians had lost their lives.) The emperor; his eldest son, a handsome, thoughtful nineteen-year-old just returned from some mysterious journey; Merek; Iskra and half a dozen tribal chiefs consumed prodigious quantities of food served by Rolph's two handsome mudders and his three younger children. Afterward they got down to the serious business of drinking long drinks and telling tall tales.

Piecing the stories together, Merek for the first time gained an idea of life on Asgard and half a dozen other planets circling around the Cepheid and two nearby suns.

There were, he gathered, ten thousand or so semi-isolated communities such as the tent city. Each had its own king, was independent so far as domestic affairs went, but paid fealty to Rolph when foreign policy was in question. Only a fraction of the five million or so barbarians lived in cities, however. The rest were broken into small tribes or family clans. Some of these herded twarks, the giant, half-tamed saurians whose meat provided the chief food staple. Others fished, hunted and did what farming was possible on planets which usually were either too hot or too cold for comfort.

A comparative few were miners, metal workers and technicians. The latter had a fairly adequate knowledge of atomic and space-warp engineering which they had managed to pick from the brains of visiting Centaurans. On the whole, however, they scoffed at complicated machinery. Like trolls or gnomes of old, they built space-ship cells in isolated cave workshops, but flatly refused to construct the roads, docks, libraries, schools, homes and amusement centers which formed the backbone of Centauran civilization.

As for weapons, they made light fusion bombs, paralysis guns and rifles and sidearms using explosive charges—for dum-dum bullets. They also had learned to operate Centauran ships and radiation cannon. But, for real satisfying carnage, they preferred swords, daggers and garrotes. As one battle-scarred chief put it after her fifth horn of mead:

"Get und' enemy guard! That barb way. Lo'g range, Centauran use big gun. Boom! Boom! Barb die quick. Sho't range, Centauran, Siriun, no like col' steel. Turn. Run. Snick!" She made a too-expressive gesture.

"What do you people know about Siriuns?" Merek marveled. "They're half a galaxy away from here."

"Too much," said Rolph, frowning at the talkative one. "There is something about a sword," he continued. "Perhaps it's a Freudian symbol of some kind. Virile, primitive peoples have won most of their victories with cold steel. Decadent races have a horror of it. Athens. Rome. Byzantium. Alexandria. They were all put to the sword!"

"Yes," Merek agreed, "and it was a desperate bayonet charge which enabled my people to capture New Chicago Airport from the Oligarchs long enough to get ships and take off for Centaurus a millennium ago."

"How many of you Centaurans would be willing to fight hand-to-hand now?"

"Uh…" Merek changed the painful subject by saying: "As I understand it, Rolph, your method of governing Barbarie is something like that used by the Iroquois Indian Federation of seventeenth century North America."

"Something like that, you antiquarian. Wasn't it George Washington who called the Iroquois 'the Romans of the New World'?" Rolph was showing off. "Well, we barbarians are the Iroquois of the Star Cluster. We conduct our lives as we please until there's fighting to be done. Then we accept iron discipline."

"And you maintain that discipline by telepathic orders?"

"After a fashion." The emperor poured another horn of mead all 'round. Iskra who had been unusually quiet all evening, seized hers and drank it at a gulp.

"That means that barbarians are dangerous enemies," said Merek, speaking to Rolph but watching the girl curiously. She seemed to be drinking heavily without getting a lift. "But what if, just once, we manage to hit you?"

"If we can manage to hang on here, we'll attack again when you weaken."

"Why are you so sure we Centaurans will crumble?"

"Amy civilization which doesn't expand—which concentrates on maintaining the status quo, as yours does—is bound to fall sooner or later. If it weren't for this Thing out here, I wouldn't risk the life of a single one of my brothers in an attack. I'd just wait a few generations for you to fall into my lap."

"I've seen no spectacular menace."

"You will, any time now. It seems bent on herding us back toward Alpha. Whenever we stay quiet a while, it gives us a jolt."

"Why don't you fight it?"

"Because my people are still mental children in many ways. They went a long way down the scale. It did things to them in addition to making them telepathic. When they can see an enemy, they joyfully fight him to the death. But the Thing can't be seen…only felt and heard. And it preys on the mind." He shook himself like a mastiff. "Let's talk of something pleasant. Have another drink and I'll get Iskra to tell you about the time she made a one-girl raid on an Arconian pleasure palace and…"

"Iskra no wanna," said the girl crossly. "Iskra col'." She shivered violently, a thing which Merek had seen no barbarian do before.

Rolph glanced sharply at his favorite, then at the hot plate. Its usual white-hot filament had turned to a dull red.

The emperor leaped to his feet, seized a fur rug from the floor and wrapped it about the girl's quaking shoulders.

"Go!" he yelled at his guests. "Thing come! Get brudder in tent. Quick!" As they scrambled upright, he added: "Iskra. Merek. Stay 'ere!"

"No!" Iskra jerked loose from his detaining hand, and stumbled toward the tent flap. "Iskra 'elp."

"I'll go with her," said Merek. "She looks sick."

"She is sick. She's unusually sensitive to a psychological attack. If she keels over, get her inside quick." Rolph pushed them through the flap, paused to zip it closed on his petrified mudders and children, then raced down the dim street with the others. They fanned out through the maze of tents, shouting warnings which were snatched away by a wind of hurricane proportions.

Iskra attempted to follow the example set by her comrades but her movements were slow and clumsy. Hardly had she run a dozen steps when she stumbled and fell headlong. The fur whipped from her bare shoulders and disappeared.

Merek picked her up like a child—a steel spring can be quite light, he discovered—then looked around for his tent. Sighting its dim outline when a shift in the wind deflected the almost solid sheet of snow for a moment, he fought doggedly toward it, in danger of losing his way at every step.

Before he reached shelter, the cold had deepened to a degree he had never experienced before. Twenty-five below and dropping several degrees a minute, he estimated, as he fought the zippered flap with stiffening fingers. It opened at last. He thrust the unconscious girl inside, followed her in a rush of blind terror and managed to seal the door behind him.

The cold within the padded walls was almost as overpowering as that in the open. He fumbled about until he found the hotplate switch. Nothing happened. Pressing his numbed fingers against the filament he could feel only a trace of warmth. He located a flashlight but it, too, refused to work. In the search he came across something even more useful—a canteen full of mead.

Stripping the girl of her ice-caked boots, kilt, mittens and helmet, he massaged her slim limbs with the fiery stuff until she moaned and protested feebly. Then he buried her under all the furs he could locate.

The exercise had served to keep him half-way warm, but when he relaxed the cold bit into him with the ferocity of a fee. He felt in his pocket for warmth tablets and swallowed three at a gulp. They helped only a little, and the pounding of his heart warned him not to increase the dose. At the same time he began to choke, as though breathing frozen coal dust. He could be dead or hopelessly frostbitten before the night was out. There was nothing for it… He dived under the furs with Iskra.

She revived after he had forced a tablet between her teeth, clung to him in a frenzy and began wailing like an infant.

"Iskra. Iskra, honey," he pleaded, stroking her curls. "There's nothing to be afraid of. Just a bad blizzard."

"No blizzard!" she chattered. "All th'g stop. Heat. Light. 'Lec-tricity… Merek 'ear win'?" He uncovered his head for a moment and listened. The night had become silent as the grave, the cold grew more intense momentarily and the blackness was like a pall. He ducked under in a panic.

Iskra's lips moved against his ear.

"Talk louder," he told her. "I can't hear you."

"Iskra shout!" The words sounded faint and far. "Brudder die outside. No can 'ear Rolph thought. Go craz'… Lissen!"

"Listen to what?" he shouted, feeling that, somehow, he must keep her talking.

"Thing speak. Say 'Oooo…ooo Iskra die, nevuh live 'gain.' Say: 'Ooo…oooo. Fee get loose. Suck bloo' aw brudder.' Merek no hear? Say 'Ha…ha…ha. Stay Omega, aw barb die quick.' Say: '…'"

"Shut up, you little fool!" He grabbed her by the shoulders and shook her until her teeth must have rattled. "You're imagining it all. I don't hear a thing. And I won't let it get you, anyway. Try to relax, child."

She snuggled her wet face against his chest and sobbed uncontrollably. He comforted her in every way he knew how. Finally she slept, cuddled up for protection against a cold which stabbed at them like knives.

* * * *

It was the Third Hour before the cold and dark lifted sufficiently to let them leave their shelter. They found a camp which looked partially sacked. Many of the tents, including Rolph's, had been flattened or blown away. Corpses of hundreds of barbarians who had been caught in, or forced into, the open, sprawled in the gutters, stiff and white as statues.

Veteran warriors stumbled about in a daze. Others, eyes staring and lips frothing, were being dragged to the hospital by luckier comrades. From the quarter which housed the mudders, children and artisans came an endless wailing.

They found Rolph standing before his wrecked tent, legs wide apart, red beard sunk on his chest. "So you survived," he said morosely. "Better men didn't."

"Bad?" Iskra patted his arm.

"Five hundred dead on Asgard alone, including both of my mudders and my two youngest," he answered with a bitter shrug. "Hundreds more gone raving mad. This can't continue." He beat his knuckles together until they dripped blood, but his eyes remained dry.

"We leave here within the week," he continued at last.

"Before our ransom arrives?" Merek's heart sank.

"Yes. We can't wait. Last night's attack was general and the worst we've had. My people can't face another. They'll scatter to their caves. That will be the end of us. Merek, you and your men will remain here. I can't risk your revealing what you know to the Centaurans just now."

"I didn't think last night was so overpowering." The admiral was sparring for time. "Bad enough yes, but nothing to start a stampede over. *I* didn't hear any voices."

"You didn't?" Rolph gripped his arm, the dawn of a strange hope in his haggard eyes. Then he shrugged. "That was because you aren't a sensitive. Telepathy can be a handicap at times."

He waved them away and resumed his meditative stance before the ruined tent.

That night Merek made a desperate gamble.

"Iskra," he said, "I saved your life last night."

"Yah." Her slim hand found his in the darkness.

"What does barbarian law say about that?" he ventured, playing a hunch based on his sketchy knowledge of mythology.

"Iskra boun' save Merek life." There was a whimper in her voice.

"Will I live long if Rolph leaves me here and the Thing comes back?"

"No. Oh no!" Her words had a double meaning. "Thing kill aw nex' ti' sure."

"You must help me escape…tonight."

"But… Iskra promise Brudder Rolph… Rolph kill Iskra… Slow."

"What does the law say?"

"Law say"—there was a sob in the darkness—"save Brudder Merek."

"Exactly. We're blood brothers now. You must save my life, but to do that you'll have to save my men, too. I can't escape alone. And you must show us where one of Rolph's old Centauran ships is berthed. You will go with us," he added gently. "Rolph will never find you."

"Rolph find," she sighed.

They crept through the gray snowstorm like shadows. Having made her decision, Iskra seemed to have no compunctions. She tried to use Rolph's name to get past the sentries at the hospital. When they hesitated and she heard them trying to get in telepathic touch with the emperor, she knifed one while Merek took care of the other.

They slipped through the quiet wards arousing the Centaurians. Fifty, they found, were still too weak to be moved. An equal number, most of them Pizarians, flatly refused to leave their warm beds when the project was explained. So there were fewer than four hundred who bundled themselves in all the furs they could find and followed their admiral out into the howling night.

"How far is this ship?" Pancrief asked after they had been breasting the gale for half an hour. With his arm still in a sling, he was finding the going hard.

"Oh, t'ree, fo' mi'," Iskra answered cheerfully as she brushed the driving snow out of her eyes. "Jus' li'l walk."

"Some of us won't make it," said the thin man. "Must be close to zero."

"Get back to the end of the line and prevent any straggling," Merek ordered. "Manfred and I will police the flanks."

As the slow minutes passed, the route began to resemble Napoleon's retreat from Moscow. Men allowed their furs to be stripped from them by the fingers of the wind. They swore. They moaned. They wept and salt tears froze to their cheeks. Many turned and, despite pleas, threats and blows, trudged back over a path which was soon obliterated by drifts. Others fell and would not move again.

"There's no fight in them," Manfred shouted across the wavering line.

"*Put* fight in them then!" Merek was belaboring a reluctant shadow with the flat of his sword. "We can't leave them here to die."

Leave them they did, nevertheless, before that nightmare journey ended. To have done otherwise would have meant the death of all. As it was, hardly a hundred men were left when, after sliding down the walls of a box canyon, they came upon the hidden ship.

Iskra beat on the entry port with the pommel of her sword.

"Oo dere?" a voice came through the vessel's loudspeaker.

"Attack start!" the girl screamed back like a Valkyrie. "Let Iskra in. 'Ave order from Brudder Rolph."

"Thor's 'ammer!" gasped the voice. "No crew 'ere. Las' ni' go Asgard 'ave fun."

"Crew come now. 'Ave mo' fun soon. Open port quick. Centauran fleet near."

The port swung wide at that and the guard appeared to peer upward apprehensively.

Iskra had her garrote ready and snared him expertly.

Merek and the half-dead Centaurans flung themselves across the threshold. Gaining strength as the warmth of the interior penetrated their bones, they scoured the ship. Three watch officers were overpowered on the bridge. A standby engineer was captured in his cabin. Within fifteen minutes the ship was won.

* * * *

As soon after takeoff as the gravitational pull of Asgard relaxed, Merek lined up his men for inspection in the littered and filthy main corridor of the old *S. S. Terra*. He got an agreeable surprise. There were plenty of frosted noses, ears, toes and fingers in the crowd, but he got an impression that the survivors were a superior lot. Well, they should be, he thought.

"Only three Second Gens in the bunch, Admiral," said Pancrief out of the corner of his mouth. He had donned a barbarian kilt, the only clothing to be found on board, and looked like an ostrich.

Merek nodded. Could it be, he wondered, that longevity had no survival value?

"Men," he said quietly, "we're half a million miles out of Asgard. Rolph has put two barb ships on our tail, but we should be able to shift into hyper before they come within range. And once in hyper, we can dodge them.

"I realize you've just taken a bad beating. I hate to give you another. I'd like to ease through hyper, but Rolph's main fleet is taking off in a day or so. We must keep ahead of it if we can and give the alarm. Those who think they can take a rough crossing, step forward."

As one man, the line moved up.

"I thought you'd say that. Very well. Strap down for hyper at 300. If anything happens to me, Captain Pancrief will take over. Captain Manfred will be next in line of command. Thank you."

"Three cheers for Admiral Merek," shouted a lanky youngster in the line.

A lump in his throat, Merek waited until the uproar died. "I wish Centaurus had ten thousand more like you," he choked at last. "Dismissed."

Rolph's ships were still only the faintest of pips on the radar when the *Terra* wrenched herself from tritium drive into space warp.

This time the green hell didn't seem quite as bad as on previous occasions. There was plenty of nausea; many of the crew suffered the usual muscle-tearing spasms. But none died and none cracked up.

"I have a notion all of us matured out on Omega," said Manfred as he, Merek, and Pancrief labored over the old-fashioned and strangely reluctant warp controls. "I feel older... And I feel good."

"How old are you?" asked Merek.

"Too damned old... Ninety-six, sir."

"Don't look forward to making your first deposit, eh?"

"No sir. Sounds awfully sentimental, I know, but you see, sir, my mother was killed in a plane crash when I was nine. I remember her well. She used to sing folksongs to me—things like 'Barbara Allen' and 'The Galactic Pioneers.' And she'd tell me stories that almost everybody has forgotten—stories of pioneer days. Guess that's why I joined the navy, sir. But," his voice shook ever so slightly, "when I deposit the memories of my first ten years, I'll forget her, and I'll forget those stories too. You might say I'll forget an important part of me. I suppose it's silly, but sometimes I think I'd rather grow old and die and be done with it."

"I know." Manfred's words brought thoughts of Merek's own youth flooding back to him: the swimming pool under the fern trees; his father's booming voice; the perfumes from the flower garden which his artist mother tended with such loving care; the peaches which his ancestors had imported from Earth and planted side by side with yar from Venus and native Merconian fruits; the sleepy reservations across the valley where the last wave of refugees had been interned. He was blessed with visual, aural and tactile memory so the scenes which flashed through his mind were almost as real as life.

"I don't mind forgetting my childhood," Pancrief put in. "My parents are divorced. I lived with my grandparents on a rundown farm. Ugh! It's that emergency deposit which burned me up."

"But I've told you about everything you forgot," Merek began.

"Everything, huh? What about the visiphone number of the girl whose picture I have in my wallet? I must have met her the day I landed on Pizar. Pretty little trick. You know her?"

Their rambling conversation was interrupted as Iskra burst onto the bridge, whistling merrily. She was not bothered, either by hyperspace or thoughts of the Bank. Even the all-pervading green murk failed to disturb her.

"Hung'?" she asked. "Iskra bri'g lunch." She put down a tray and held it firmly to protect it from the ship's lurches. "Iskra cook goo'."

"Take it away," groaned Pancrief. "Cooked goo has no appeal."

"W'y ship go slow?" She hopped onto Merek's desk and sat swinging her legs, little-girl fashion. Now that she had had a bath—Merek had given it to her, despite kicks and screams—she looked, and smelled, pretty enough to kiss.

"Ship go fast," the admiral mimicked her. "Any faster and every soul on board would be turned inside out."

"Huh!" she jeered. "Rolph fix ship. Go plenty mo' fas'. Iskra show."

She made a grab for a lever which protruded from a crudely-chopped hole in the main control panel.

Merek caught her arm just in time, his heart in his mouth. "Easy, woman!" he yelled.

"No woman! Girl!"

"Sorry. Have it your way. But stay away from those controls."

"Aw ri'." She was sulking now. "Merek be sorry." She snatched up the rejected tray and stalked out, miraculously keeping her balance on the wobbly deck.

"What a wench," Pancrief admired. "But what are you going to do with the little hellcat when we get home?"

"*If* we get home." Merek resumed his balancing of the nicked and grimy controls.

"If I may say so, sir," Manfred said after a time, "you—we may have made a mistake in not letting her explain what that lever is for."

"I was a fool." Merek rose groggily. "I'll go talk to her."

But when he found her, playing craps with the barbarian prisoners, Iskra refused to talk. "Too late now," she shrugged crossly.

* * * *

The *Terra* popped out of hyper just five days after she had plunged in, to break the record for the Omega run. The white fires of Alpha lay dead ahead. Arcon, outermost of the main planets, was almost too close for comfort. Mercon sparkled green in the middle distance. Beacon, red as a spotlight, could just be seen as it prepared to start its yearly plunge between Alpha I and II. Pizar was occluded by faraway Proxima.

Merek took the minds of his crew members off their aches and pains by setting them to cleaning ship. Then he started warming up the tritium drive and the communicator. Contacting the inter-planetary transmitter on Mercon, he asked to be put through to the Council.

"Ether's jammed with high priority stuff," the operator frowned. "Who're you?"

"Rear Admiral Merek, escaped from Omega."

There was a wait of many seconds while his words winged their way across millions of miles of space.

"Sorry, sir." The operator saluted briskly. "Welcome home. I'll put Her Intelligence on at once." His nondescript face faded from the screen, to be replaced by a view of Marian's library. The secretary was seated there, her lovely body tense as she leaned forward, waiting for the call.

"Merek reporting," he said, pulses pounding at his first face-to-face meeting with the wisest and most beautiful woman in the universe. "I escaped from Asgard on the remodeled merchantman *S. S. Terra* with one hundred of my men and ten prisoners. Rolph's fleet is close behind. Prepare for an attack in force."

Until his words crossed the void her face remained unchanged. He had a chance to look into those fathomless eyes under brows which slanted upward questioningly; the high cheek bones and the dimple which played at the left corner of those lovely lips.

"Rolph and his fleet landed on Beacon two days ago," she said at last. "They must have some way of getting through the warp almost instantaneously. Our fleet is on its way. Make contact with Admiral Mendez and take over command from him at once. Understood?"

"But, Your Intelligence," he ventured to protest. "I have no idea what has been going on in recent weeks. Admiral Mendez..."

"Mendez is not yet fully recovered from his fractured skull. He is in no condition to command." Her voice was bitter.

"Well, there must be many more experienced officers than I." He was perspiring freely under that steady, appraising gaze.

"That's the trouble, Merek. They have experience but lack imagination. You are the only man we have who can possibly match wits with Rolph."

"Very well, Your Intelligence."

"One thing more. Land your crew at Arcon with orders that they deposit their experiences on Omega before reporting to the fleet for reassignment."

Merek licked lips which had suddenly gone stiff.

"I am sorry, Intelligence," he managed at last. "I cannot obey that order."

Utter astonishment spread over her face. Probably, this was the first time she had ever been crossed. "Did I hear you correctly?"

"You did."

"It is the law promulgated by the Council, for the safety of all Centaurans."

"I know. But I need the experience my men accumulated at Omega. I refuse to have that background pried out of their minds by a bank teller!"

"Background of defeat!"

"Perhaps!" His eyes clashed with hers. "Nevertheless, they will receive no deposit orders from me. If you wish my resignation..."

Suddenly she laughed, a ringing peal which set off harmonics in the mike.

"I like you, brash Merek. You're the first man who has dared say 'No' to me in a century. I could have you shot for refusing to obey orders. Perhaps I will, later. In the meantime, good luck, Admiral. And good hunting on Beacon."

CHAPTER X

It was a broken Mendez who piped his successor aboard the *Alpha*. His left cheek twitched. His bark was muted. The other officers who gathered at the conference table also showed signs of strain.

"W-welcome to your new command, Admiral Merek," stuttered the former great man. "Your q-quarters have been prepared. We await y-your orders."

Merek looked around the table from the twittery Mendez to the pompous Marlborough, the phlegmatic Anderson, the sulky Pierce (restored to command out of grim necessity) and half a dozen captains, all of them Second Gens, naturally.

"Each of you will keep his present post," he said at last. "I will remain aboard the *Terra* with Captains Pancrief and Manfred as my aides."

"That heap of scrap?" Mendez exploded. "It isn't fit for the junkheap."

"I have good reasons for operating in this manner. The first is that the *Terra* has been tampered with in a way which I must investigate. In the second place, I have about decided that we cannot continue to fight Rolph at long range. He is a guerilla fighter with a number of great advantages on his side, including telepathic control of his crews, the apparent ability to dodge in and out of hyper at will, and some method of making his ships invisible which I do not fully comprehend.

"On the other hand, when he operates in this system he is forced to do something which he does not want to do—that is, set up a base where he can establish fuel and ammunition dumps, hospitals and food depots. Our only hope, as I see it, is to destroy that base before he cam consolidate and fortify it. If we can do this, I think we can contain him. But if he continues to hold Beacon, nothing can keep him from moving against Arcon, Mercon and Pizar."

"A landing on Beacon?" spluttered Marlborough. "Impossible!"

"Why?" Merek stared the florid man down.

"In a few weeks no Centauran can live on that planet. Why man, Beacon's mean temperature stands above 150 degrees Fahrenheit during the three months when it passes between Alpha I and II. We'd be roasted."

"The barbarians evidently don't intend to roast. Scientists have lived on Beacon during opposition. I think we can survive if we have the guts."

"What is your plan?" Anderson spoke for the first time.

"Our only chance is to make the quickest possible run to Beacon, ray the base, crash-land if necessary, before Rolph's clumsy ships can rally, dismount our heaviest cannon, deploy them under cover and use them to keep him from following us in. That will give us a breathing spell during which the Pizarian shipyards can complete our third fleet. With the new ships, and the knowledge I have gained regarding Rolph's method of infighting, we can lick him."

"Nonsense," muttered Mendez. "We can't win."

"I'm for giving Merek's plan a try," said Pierce.

For once the others voted with the Pizarian.

* * * *

The twenty-million-mile run to blistered little Beacon was made at top constant acceleration despite the intense discomfort occasioned by life under a steady pressure of 5G's. Iskra hated it especially because of the way it made her facial muscles sag into a caricature of old age and her dancing feet drag like leaden weights.

"Why Merek no push lever?" she demanded as she pointed toward the jerry-built contraption on the control panel. "Reach Beacon no ti'. Zip!"

"Go into hyperspace here?" Merek was aghast. "Even if that gadget does what you say it will, we'd smash into something or be a light year off-course before I could return the lever to neutral. In addition, the ship would expand to infinite size, if unified field math means anything at all, and the whole system would go nova."

"No," she said firmly. "'Urt li'l bit. Dat aw."

"My dear wo—My dear girl," he patronized, "are you aware of the tremendous power needed to warp space? Let me put it this way: Einstein and his successors say that space is curved because of the matter it contains. In fact, the universe is a closed curve, like a vast balloon, with the galaxies, stars and planets scattered over its surface. Suppose you want to pinch the two sides of that balloon so that, say, Alpha Centauri and Omega Centauri come close together, instead of being 20,000 light years apart. Have you any conception of the energy required, and the infinite care needed, to perform that maneuver?"

"'Ave gum?" yawned Iskra, taking a stick out of her pocket and frugally breaking it in half. (She had developed a passion for the ancient delicacy which was unknown on Omega.) When Merek accepted, she clambered laboriously onto a desk and sat regarding him like a prematurely aged imp. "Merek nut," she continued after she had chewed for a while. "Space no like dat."

"What?" he yelled.

"Space close' curve, su'," she went on calmly. "W'at inside?"

"Why, uh," he blinked, "there's nothing inside of the space-time continuum, I suppose. What's that got to do with it?"

"If nuttin' inside dis room—jus' nuttin'—den walls go like dis, no?" She pressed the palms of her hands together.

"Why yes, I guess you're right. If there were *absolutely* nothing, not even space, between the walls, they would have to coincide." He regarded her with new respect. Was he on the verge of discovering Rolph's greatest secret?

"Space like dat," she insisted. "Go through, all star, planet, galaxy, 'mos' touch, like dis." She clenched her fist. "Centauran fool. Try warp space w'en nuttin' to warp. Waste power. Go slow. Get sick. Barb jus' open door. Step through. Zip! Merek try. Jus' push li'l lever."

"How does a kid like you know all this?" He stared at her in awe.

"Aw barb know aw t'ing any barb know," she answered, masticating enthusiastically. "Know aw Centauran know, too," she added, jolting him to his toes. "Centauran no know much. Rolph study lo' ti'. Mighty smart. Fix Centauran hyper drive goo'."

"I'll say. But, if I push that lever, and it works, this ship will leave the rest of my fleet 'way behind." He studied her with a dawning suspicion. "Then, when we got to Beacon, Rolph would be waiting to gobble us up. Right?"

"No!" Her face flaming with anger, she jumped from her perch, then gasped as her feet hit the deck with a bang. "Rolph no know Merek come." She rubbed her ankles to take the sting out.

"Why not?" He gripped her shoulders. "You're a barb, aren't you? And you're telepathic."

"Iskra no tell Rolph," she whimpered. "Merek save Iskra life. Blood brudder. Iskra no hurt. Is law."

"All right," he relented. "But be careful you don't broadcast by accident."

"Rolph ask Iskra kill Merek," she went on demurely. "Two day since. 'Fore Rolph 'ave go back Omega."

Here was news indeed! Interplanetary telepathy! And Rolph not at Beacon!

"And what did you answer?" What an eternal ass he had been to give this wild girl the run of the ship!

"Iskra no answer. No fool. Rolph get fix. Come grab Merek."

The conversation gave Merek plenty of food for thought as the painful days dragged along. Now he knew that the secret of Rolph's hyperspace maneuverability had been built into the *Terra*. The barbarian's telepathy worked at interplanetary distances, but not through the warp. It was directional. It could be blocked at will. The emperor was not expecting an immediate counterattack or he would not have returned to Omega.

His heart sang. There was a chance of victory—just a chance—providing Iskra did not become annoyed at him and forget that they were "brudders."

* * * *

The Centauran ships shrieked down on Beacon with guns blazing at maximum diffusion. For once they caught the barbarians flatfooted, with all their attention fixed on constructing the sheet metal warehouses, machine shops and other buildings of the base. There was no answering fire. When they landed, only masses of charred bodies greeted them.

"Too easy, Merek," was Pancrief's lugubrious comment. "Much too easy."

The five thousand or so Centaurans sweated out the next week getting the big guns and their atomic generators out of the ships and mounted in concealed positions around the circumference of the arid planet. The cloudless skies were like brass at all hours, for no sooner did Alpha I set then Alpha II rose to take its place. Hourly the heat increased as Beacon prepared for her fiery dive between the two stars. The orbit of Beacon was a complicated figure eight which encompassed each star in turn. Arcon and Mercon, lying out much farther, circled both suns and therefore were never subjected to a similar test.

Only the fact that Beacon's gravitational pull was negligible kept the grumbling sailors at their tasks. Few except the veterans on the *Terra* showed sincere devotion to the Centauran cause. The latter vividly remembered the beating they had taken at Omega and were out to revenge it, even if they were dehydrated in the process.

And Iskra accomplished wonders in keeping up their morale. They loved her wink and the tilt of her little gray kilt. They adopted her as their mascot, not only because she was always ready to haul on a line or help put up camouflage nets, but also because she entertained them, during the rest periods when it was too hot to rest, by doing naughty Highland flings or singing bloodthirsty sagas.

She even taught them swordplay of a sort, and the use of more modern hand weapons salvaged from the virtually undamaged warehouses. She also showed the pharmacist's mates how to mix a concoction which took some of the devilish bite out of the heat.

Crews of the other ships sometimes gathered 'round to watch Merek's crewmen cutting, slashing, tossing grenades and experimenting with the archaic rifles and automatics while Iskra sweated, shouted instructions and praised outstanding performers. But, when the admiral proposed that they, too, join in the sport, they drifted away to raid the plentiful supplies of mead stored in the warehouses.

As one somewhat effete Arconian engineer put it: "It's bad enough to have to fight those barbarian scum, but I draw the line on imitating them!"

The other officers were slow to recognize the value of such exercises but they finally joined their pleas to Merek's, to small avail. Finally orders were issued. The men obeyed by waving swords around and tinkering a bit with the other weapons, but they still put their faith in long range, bloodless combat. Instead of perfecting themselves in the enemy's fighting techniques they quarreled, gambled, drank heavily and went rapidly to pieces in this corner of hell's kitchen.

When no reinforcements had arrived by the end of a fortnight, Merek took the chance of calling Marian on a scrambled circuit.

"I must have ten thousand fresh troops at once, Your Intelligence," he told her firmly. "I can't be responsible for holding this position unless I get help."

"I'm sorry, Merek," she answered wistfully. "You seem to have been too successful. The people love you. They are erecting statues in your honor here. But few of them volunteer to die for you."

"Draft them then," he snarled.

"The Council has proposed a universal draft law, but the people must vote on it. Don't forget, Centauran democratic tradition goes back a thousand years."

"The law requiring emergency deposits wasn't voted on."

"I wish it had been." He couldn't see her through the scramble, of course, but he thought there were tears in her voice. "It was a mistake. I see that now. Forgetfulness has made the people overconfident. Past defeats mean little to them now that we have scored one victory. And since you seem to be doing all right out there, they see little reason why they should blister their soft skins rushing to your assistance."

"How many men *can* you send me at once?"

"I don't dare weaken the defenses of Mercon and Arcon. That means there's only the police force available... About five thousand men in all."

"Get them here!"

"Are you giving me orders, Merek?" There were knives in her voice again.

"I'm giving you good advice, woman! Advice which may save our system!"

"I don't have ships to send such a force."

"Commandeer the passenger liners on the interplanetary runs."

"That would take weeks."

"It should have been done months ago! Is the Council asleep?"

"You insolent young puppy. I..."

"Take it or leave it," he interrupted. "I'll send my ships to you under Mendez for use as transports. There'll be danger of a mutiny here soon, if the men have any way of getting home. Load them quick if your value *your* soft skin. Send cops—robots—even Councilmen—anything you can scrape up. But *send* 'em!" He cut the circuit.

"Scrambler didn't work so good, did it?" said Pancrief the next "day" as they stood at the sun-drenched base watching the disarmed ships marshalling for the flight home. As he spoke a dozen burnished, copper-colored globes materialized in the sky! Rolph had returned from Omega.

"The emp seems to have shipped some new heavy stuff," was Pancrief's acid comment as beams of blue radiance lashed out from several of the ships.

Before the Centauran vessels could be gotten under way by their skeleton crews, most of them were slanting down toward Beacon, hulled in dozens of places and out of control. Only the *Alpha* was allowed to limp away.

"What's the matter with *our* guns?" Merek yelled.

Instantly his answer came. From emplacements scattered among the rocky hills, radiation snatched at the barbarian ships. Three of them blazed into incandescence. (The fragile, titanium hull of even the most powerful warship could withstand a direct hit for seconds only.)

Before the beams could center on other craft, the latter exploded of their own volition. Swarms of fragments glittered in the sunlight for a moment, then vanished. With nothing sizeable left to shoot at, the Centauran beams wavered and cut off.

"Arm yourselves with hand weapons," Merek bellowed as he raged among the warehouses and the huddling, terrified Centaurans. "Pancrief, see that swords, rifles and machine guns are distributed. Anderson!" He shook the Arconian out of a semi-stupor. "Throw a cordon around the base... Here you!" He grabbed a petrified lieutenant. "Find Marlborough. Tell him I said to get his men digging trenches, throwing up barricades. On the double!"

Gradually, some sort of order was restored. As the self-propelled cells out of which the barbarian space ships had been assembled drifted to the ground in a wide circle around the base a ragged battle line was formed. Marlborough, puffing and blowing, deployed his crews among the sand dunes to the south of the warehouse cluster. Anderson took the cliffs to the west. Pierce scattered a detachment of would-be machine gunners through some scrub in the eastern valley. Merek, Pancrief, Manfred and their handful of veterans took shelter along the flanks of the *S. S. Terra*. This ship, which had been too small to be worth using as a transport, still lay on the sand north of base and partially blocked a continuation of the eastern valley which was free of brush and seemed to invite attack.

Hardly had the lines been set up when the barbs emerged from the protection of their cells, formed loose companies around their tribal standards and waited, shouting insults, for the order to attack.

"There's Rolph," said Pancrief, who was lying in a hastily-dug foxhole beside his chief. He pointed to where the emperor's red head towered above those of his men. "Shame the *Terra* doesn't mount any cannon."

"Rolph feel goo'," grunted Iskra from Merek's other side.

"Merek!" The emperor bellowed through cupped hands. "Do you surrender, or do I have to come and get you?"

"Come get me," Merek shouted back.

The barbarians roared. They liked the Centauran and they liked a fight.

Rolph lifted his two-handed sword. His warriors emptied their rifles at the foxholes in front of the grounded ship. Then they threw them away, snatched up automatics and bags of hand grenades and lunged forward in a roaring, apparently undisciplined mob.

"Rolph make mistake," Iskra shouted over the outlandish racket. "More good strike at Marlborough. Sof' line dere."

"Shhh! Don't even think that! He may hear you!" Merek, too, had been fretting about the rear. He hugged a rifle awkwardly and fired burst after burst of the barbarians' own dum-dums at the sprinting emperor. Dodging; seeking cover where there was any; crawling over the tops of dunes to avoid being silhouetted against the sky, the giant came on, though men fell screaming on all sides of him.

The veterans of the Omega expedition, small in number though they were, put on a good show. They fired slowly, getting a man with each murderous bullet. Long before they came within grenade range, the fur-clad warriors wavered. As casualties became unbearable they turned and fled.

A sailor, posted on top of the ship, began to blare the good news to the camp through a loudspeaker. Cheers rang out behind the embattled company.

"Rolph mad now," Iskra reported, eyes shining. "Big fight come."

"Pancrief, get back and warn them," snapped Merek. Then to the girl: "Doesn't Rolph have any heavier guns?"

"Comin' up, brudder. Take ti' get ready."

Almost at once the characteristic burp of bazookas made itself heard. The Centaurans began to suffer their first casualties as shells burst among them.

Working around the circle of trenches, doing his best to encourage the other officers and their quaking men, Merek found time to marvel at the primitive nature of the fighting. In their enthusiasm over radiation beams, his people had always scorned the use of messy small arms. On the other hand, barbarian weapons were only refinements of twentieth century stuff which they had found in books salvaged from Earth.

Soon after he returned to his sun-baked post near the *Terra*, the entire barb line began to move. This time the warriors were cautious; they crawled forward like Indians under cover of a bazooka barrage.

Somewhat to Merek's surprise, the Centaurans stood fast and did a fair amount of execution with rifles which they quickly learned how to use.

The attack dribbled away. The defenders cheered briefly, then grew silent as a new flock of cells made its appearance overhead. They expected to be bombed from the air but the cells passed over and landed in a circle around the emperor's twark-tail standard.

"Rolph no want spoil supply base," Iskra answered Merek's unspoken question. Then she drew in her breath sharply. "Fee come in cell. Bad!"

"What do they use the fees for?" asked Pancrief, who had just returned from his rounds to report all quiet.

Before she could answer, the brush parted to reveal the most outlandish sight the Pizarian had ever witnessed. Half a hundred barbarians, mounted on as many of the pale yellow insects which Merek had hunted on Asgard, came charging up the valley toward them.

Because of Beacon's low gravity, the creatures seemed little handicapped by their riders, who clung to some sort of harness on the bulbous, hairy bodies. They approached with the speed of dreams in twenty foot leaps.

Merek's little band cursed but did not waver. Each fired until the gun scorched his hands or jammed. At closer range, grenades created green-spattered havoc. And, when the survivors still came on, the Centaurans leaped out of their foxholes and met the nightmare steeds with cold steel.

Iskra showed them how to do it. Ducking in and out of the ruck, she dodged the dripping palps and mandibles and the blows aimed at her by the riders while she slashed at the tips of those awful legs with her sword. Cheering her to the echo, the men followed their mascot's example. Apparently this was the one attack the fee cavalry could not cope with. In a twinkling the twenty or so barbarians remaining were dismounted and fighting, back to back, for their lives.

The defenders' experience at swordplay served them in good stead now. Wild with fury at what they considered a sneak attack, they leaped over, dived under or went through the living wall. And the warriors died to a man.

Merek was dripping blood from several light wounds before it was over and he could shout to the ship's lookout for information on the rest of the battle.

"Not so good, sir," the sailor called down. "The rest of the line's rolled back to the warehouses—what's left of it. They didn't know what to make of those yellow varmints. Don't think they can hold much longer. We're cut off."

"Men," said Merek to his sweating, panting crew, "if we lose Beacon we're done for. The other planets can't be held long if Rolph gets a foothold here. I don't ask the impossible. There are only eighty of you left on your feet. If you say so, we'll take the *Terra* up and go for help. But if you'll follow me, we can take the barbs in the rear and give 'em what for. How about it?"

"Let's go!" yelled a sailor who was covered from head to foot with the green ichor of a slaughtered fee. "I said it before and I say it again. Three cheers for Admiral Merek."

They grabbed up their guns and as much ammunition and as many grenades as they could carry. They started for the group of warehouses at a ragged double.

Pandemonium reigned inside the compound. The hollow crash of grenades exploding within sheet metal walls mingled with shrieks of the wounded and dying and the hoarse yells of the victory-glutted barbarians.

The sailors followed Iskra, Pancrief and Merek down the single street. (Where was Manfred? the admiral found a split second in which to wonder.) They laid a wall of hot lead before them. Rolph's men, engaged in closing a solid ring of steel around their crumbling foes, howled like wolves as they tried to turn and meet this unexpected assault.

And Iskra went berserk again. Her eyes stared. When her grenades were exhausted, she drew her bloody sword and swung it like a maniac. Froth formed at the corners of her mouth and whipped away in the hot, smoke-filled wind as she sang:

> *"Tempered and sharpened*
> *On far Omega*
> *Come now wi't Merek*
> *To take goo' revenge.*
> *Make way fo' de lightnin'.*
> *Run far from de thunder.*
> *No barb dare face Merek.*
> *Rolph day now be done!"*

Her companions took up the chant until it swelled high above the other battle noises. They formed a wedge and bored in…in…in…until it seemed that the Amazon's prophecy might come true. The barbarians, who had spent their first fury, could not stand before them. They gave back grudgingly.

The other crews took heart and rallied. Merek saw Anderson swinging a crowbar as though it were a tooth pick. Pierce and a few of his men gained the roof of the largest warehouse and began hurling grenades into the ruck.

The Centaurans' ammunition was exhausted now and, anyway, the press was too tight for anything but infighting. With Merek flanking Iskra on the right and Pancrief on the left, the dwindling flying wedge bucked ahead. No one stood long before their dripping blades—until Rolph fought his way around a corner and barred their way.

"No furder!" He spoke as though lecturing children.

Iskra, like a feminine David, struck at the barbarian Goliath with all the force of her berserk insanity. He parried, reversed in mid-swing and slashed at her throat. She just managed a riposte and continued on with a catlike molinet aimed at the emperor's eyes. He sprang back with an agility almost incredible for one of his size—escaped with a cut that laid his cheek open to the bone.

But, her first rush over, Iskra found herself overmatched by her stronger and heavier opponent. She fought savagely, though it soon became evident that Rolph was playing her, like a game fish on a line.

"Iskra surrender, no die," he said once.

She spat in his face and launched a blow at his hip which sent him leaping backward again.

That attack proved her undoing. Her foot slipped in a pool of blood as she tried to follow her advantage. Rolph struck as coldly as a surgeon wielding a scalpel.

As the broadsword whistled down, Merek shot out his own blade to deflect it. The force of the blow drove him to his knees, but he managed to get in front of the sagging girl.

"Coward!" he raged. "Your life or mine, Rolph."

"Sorry!" Rolph showed his white teeth in what was meant for a grin. "I forgot she was your girl. We don't"—he caught a stinging blow on his hilt—"have time"—he lashed out like a demon—"for chivalry"—he too slipped, but recovered—"out among the star clusters."

Thrust and parry! Slash and dodge! There was no finesse to the combat. It raged so fiercely that, all about, barbarians and Centaurans stopped to watch and even to cheer. Merek thanked his stars for the training with edged weapons which Iskra had given him. A fencer would have been dead long ere this.

He realized that he was no match for the red-bearded giant. So far he had managed to escape injury, but he had inflicted no wounds and, momentarily, he felt strength leaking away through his fingertips.

"For Iskra!" he panted, putting every ounce of the strength which remained in one last despairing blow at that horned helmet which swam before him.

Rolph had no time to parry, or perhaps disdained to do so.

He, too, brought his sword down with all the force of his mighty arms.

* * * *

Merek regained consciousness to find a battered and bandaged Pancrief trying to feed him mead with a spoon.

"Thank God you're awake!" The Pizarian's larynx bobbed like a cork.

"What happened?" Merek tried to sit up in the narrow bunk, but thought better of it.

"Your crash helmet proved to be made of harder stuff than the fancy thing Rolph was wearing."

"He's...?"

"Quite dead."

"And the others... Manfred...?"

"He'll never worry again about forgetting his mother."

"Marlborough, Anderson, Pierce?"

"Anderson's alive, but will never fight again. The rest are dead, sir."

"How did we escape?"

"Rolph's son took command when his father fell. He gave us safe conduct to the *Terra*—the hundred and fifty odd who were left—more than half of them our own boys, you'll be proud to know, sir." Pancrief's long face was working strangely. "The barbs lined up, their swords at salute, and cheered us as we collected our wounded, entered the ship and took off."

"And they hold Beacon?"

"They hold Beacon."

"Where are we now?"

"Coming in for a landing at Mercon City. I pushed Iskra's lever, like she showed me once when you weren't looking..." The captain began to blubber. "It worked just fine."

"And Iskra?" The dread question could not be put off any longer.

"Dying, sir. She's conscious, but in no pain."

"Take me to her." He sat up, conquered his dizziness and allowed Pancrief to help him to his feet.

"Hi, Brudder Merek." The girl winked gravely as he entered her cabin. Chest swathed in bandages through which bright blood was seeping, she was half-sitting in her bunk, propped up by many pillows. They had washed her pale face. She looked utterly feminine and lovely as she stretched out one hand. "Come say goo'by Iskra."

"Oh, now," he began. "You're not..." He was stopped by the look in her eyes.

"Dark come soon, mebbe so like in tent," she said after she had held his hand for a long time. "Kiss Iskra 'gain, like dat ti'."

He pressed trembling lips to her firm cold ones.

"No cry, brudder," she whispered. "No 'urt to die."

"Don't," he begged. And then he lied because he thought it would please her. "I love you, Iskra."

"No," she smiled. "Merek no love Iskra. Different from girl on Mercon. Too much like boy—like brudder. Dat goo', too."

"No," he choked. "I…"

"Iskra die now," she interrupted. "Be born 'gain soon. Be great warrior, mebbe so." She turned her face to the cabin wall and added faintly, "No fun… Merek…not…dere."

"Iskra," he raged. "You can't quit like this!"

"Iskra no quit." She stirred restlessly. "Jus' res' li'l bit."

"Quitter!" he taunted, fighting back his sobs. "Here we are, coming in for a landing on Mercon. The best doctors in the universe will be waiting to come aboard and help you. An'," he shifted into the patois in his desperate effort to reach her fading spirit, "Iskra curl up like sick twark…jus' w'en Brudder Merek need mos'!"

"Merek *need* Iskra?" She turned her head to look at him in astonishment.

"Su'," he improvised madly. "Mebbe so, Thing come Mercon soon. Merek need Iskra 'elp 'im fight."

"Oh." She took a long, shuddering breath. "Den 'old Iskra 'and."

When the doctors were dragged into the cabin by Pancrief an hour later, they found the two lying unconscious together, hands locked in a grip which was hard to break.

CHAPTER XI

A week later Merek had sufficiently recovered from his head wound to face one of the rare gatherings of the full Centauran Council. Still weak and subject to dizzy spells, he was allowed the privilege of sitting in the presence of those august personages who guided the destinies of three billion people.

The many-pillared room, filled with sunlight and flowers, gave no hint of the doom which was creeping upon three planets. The councilors, dressed in the simple white robes of their office, sat like Roman senators on folding curial chairs, their backs to an animated, tri-dimensional mural of the Centauran solar system.

Those present included Anthony of Arcon, the physicist; Merton, the famous archeologist; Poynetz, the Pizarian philosopher; Martin, the economist; half a dozen other Arconian and Merconian geniuses whose names Merek's tired mind refused to recall; white-haired but otherwise hale and hearty Arthur Franklin, Council President and last man alive of the first generation of Centauran pioneers, and finally Marian, historian and secretary of the gathering.

Merek had eyes only for the latter. She was far more serenely beautiful than he had imagined, for no visi-screen could do her justice. She was the epitome of his dreams of fair women. An ancient quotation drifted through his bemused mind: "She could actually hear the great stars in heaven, speaking from their motion and brightness, saying things perfectly to the cosmos." Well, it was too late now. He was pledged to a wild woman from Omega.

He managed to take a firm grip on his thoughts and finally concluded his report:

"We captured Beacon but could not hold it," he said. "If I still have your confidence, I will lead another expedition there as soon as more warships are completed. If not, I hereby tender my resignation."

"Merek did a magnificent job with the forces available." Marian's smile warmed his aching heart.

"True." Franklin spoke as though the weight of his endless years bore heavily upon him. "So let us not speak of resignations...nor of expeditions."

"My men stand ready to fight to the death," Merek cried.

"Your *young* men do, perhaps," Franklin corrected. "But the Second Gens, and even those persons who have made only a few memory deposits, failed you, and will continue to fail you. Is it not so?"

The admiral stood mute.

"Moreover," the old, old man went on gently, "recent emergency deposits have disoriented even the youngest elements. Totally unprepared for defeat, they have now developed serious neuroses which no further deposits can cure. For all or these reasons, the majority of the Council has agreed that the Bank is a failure."

"The Bank has given us the highest type of civilization known to exist," Poynetz stayed true to Pizarian rebel form by commenting acidly. "And it has given us immortality."

"Not true immortality." Franklin's voice rang with a sort of anger. "It has no survival value. We are being overwhelmed by a lower form of culture. Our epitaph will be that we dreamed immortality but were unable to achieve it."

"Perhaps," ventured a Pizarian sociologist, "barbarian civilization has risen higher than ours. They have developed telepathy, Admiral Merek says, and an amazing ability to adapt themselves to hyperspace and other hostile environments. I..." He stopped in confusion, conscious of the horrified stares of other Councilors. Here was a conception which their proud minds automatically rejected.

"Nonsense," said Franklin. "Nevertheless, we are not now, and probably never will be, in a position to defend ourselves from the Omegan horde. Egypt, Greece, Carthage, Rome, Spain, Britain and other terrestrial civilizations fell fighting and were ground to powder because they refused to admit their decadence. We shall be wiser than they. We shall bow before the barbarians and ask their mercy. In that way some part, at least, of our culture may survive."

"Is there no other way, Your Intelligence?" cried Merek, whose wound had begun to pound again. "I have been on Omega. I have seen its filth and berserk brutality. The barbarians will show us no mercy. I would gladly die to prevent them ravening across my homeland."

"Would enough others die with you?" the president demanded. "The people are begging for peace at any price. I am embarrassed when they kneel before me in the streets, embrace my knees, kiss my hands and beg me to let the barbarians come, if necessary, to prevent their death."

"There must be a way. There has to be one." Merek struggled to his feet and gripped the platinum railing before the dais until his knuckles showed white.

"Do you know what it is?" It was Marian who leaned forward and spoke.

"It may still not be too late to make some sort of alliance with the barbs against the Thing they fear on Omega. There must be thousands of habitable planets in that star cluster, with room enough for all."

"Wishful thinking, my boy," said Franklin. "It is too late."

"Let me try to find some other solution, then."

There was a whispered consultation among the Councilors.

"We grant you three months," Franklin said at last. "Yesterday the Council signed a truce of that length with Rolphson. As a result, the new emperor has withdrawn from Beacon to Asgard to await our formal surrender."

"Perhaps Beacon became too hot, even for barbarians," Merek gritted.

"Perhaps. At least we have a three-month breathing spell."

"Will you help me to find a way of escape? And give me authority to follow it if there is a chance of success?"

Something akin to hope was reborn on the dais.

"We will all help you," Marian answered, placing her hand over his clenched fist.

"Very well then." He snapped the droop out of his shoulders. "I would like to return to my home to think and to recover from this wound. I want to take my crew, my prisoners, and the ship I captured on Omega. I think I can induce the barbarians"—he meant Iskra but could not quite bring himself to say so—"to explain the ways in which they have altered the *S. S. Terra*. There are hospitals and rest homes near my village where my men can recover their health and spirits. Finally, I must feel free to consult any member of the Council at any time. If I find what I am looking for, we will have to act instantly."

"Agreed," said Franklin. "You are our only hope now, son."

The enormity of what he had done struck Merek full in the face as he walked down the marble stairs. He, a youngster not yet in the prime of life, had been given carte blanche by the greatest minds of the age on his half-promise to save civilization—and he hadn't an idea of how to proceed.

Well! He breathed deeply. It was spring again. The dreaming city was one mass of bloom. Smiling, tall...decadent...men and women strolled barefoot along the grass-covered streets as though a world was not ending. He loved the placid city. A shame if the barbarians put it to the torch, but nothing that hadn't happened thousands of times when contented people forgot that eternal vigilance is the price of liberty!

Contented people? Remembering the woman he had seen during his first landing on Asgard, he pondered whether many Centaurans might not welcome a little carnage to vary the tenor of their uneventful, endless lives. Maybe Centaurus was slowly boring itself to death. He must investigate that angle the next time he talked to Marian. Humming an old tune, he strode toward the nearest visi-booth to make arrangements for his home-coming.

* * * *

Merekton, which his family had colonized—and named with typical pioneer lack of imagination—was balm to Merek's wounded body and spirit for the first week or so after his arrival. It was good to hear his father's booming voice as they tramped the hills or sat under drooping fern trees beside the lake and discussed an encyclopedia of zoology on which the older man was working. It was good to have his artist mother fuss over him. It was good to see the wide-eyed hero worship with which his sister Matilda, a serious-minded adolescent, regarded him. It was even good to meet again his grandparents, great-grandparents, great-great-grandparents and a host of other smiling, soft-voiced relatives of varying degrees of "greatness" who still lived on the ancestral homestead. Most of them he had almost forgotten, but still it was good to have them welcome him back from the stars.

Yet, as the lazy days passed, Merek began to feel a vague discontent. He fretted about Iskra, though frequent reports from the spaceport hospital assured him that she would recover. Then he could not ignore the fact that his parents had lost all recollection of his childhood days. He had been born when they were in their nineties. Now, when he himself had reached fifty, they had made four Bank deposits at the regular ten-year intervals and therefore could remember him only as they had known him when he had grown to manhood. It was disheartening to make some reference to an incident in his early youth only to be met by polite, uncomprehending stares. Only with Matilda did he have any real continuity.

"I feel rootless," he told Pancrief one evening as they sat watching the sunsets from the veranda of the rest-home bar.

"I know," answered the captain. "I never go home any more if I can dodge it." He nodded to a pair of crew members as they climbed the veranda steps. "Of course my grandparents try to make me feel comfortable. They even read up on diaries they kept during my boyhood. But it's no good." He downed his drink, then grimaced. "I think that big lug behind the bar is putting water in the Scopio. Wish I had a horn of mead. Boy, that stiff had a real kick, didn't it."

"It sure did," sighed one of the newcomers. "You know, those barbs may be full of fleas, but they sure know how to make liquor."

"Isn't there anything to *do* around this dump, Admiral?" asked his pug-nosed companion. "I've rested, swum and stuffed myself until I'm about to go bats."

"Aren't the girls treating you right, Allison?" Pancrief grinned.

"Girls!" exploded the one who had spoken first. "The girls around here remind me of beautiful dolls. They go sweeping around all covered up in those fluttery robes. They're polite to a man, but they only want to talk about things like advanced art and the latest visidrama!" Words failed him.

"Give me one of those barb amazons any day—or night," Allison agreed, his eyes brightening. "If you don't object, sir..." He looked at Merek. "I'd like to tell you about one I met. She stood six feet tall in her boots, but..."

"Not now, Lieutenant," said Merek as he noted a disapproving frown on the face of the hovering bartender. "Yes," he said to that worthy, "another drink all 'round." To the others he added: "If you're bored, why don't you pay a visit to the reservation? It's not far from here."

"The reservation?" asked pug-nose. (What was his name? thought Merek. Oh yes, it was Pound.) "You mean where they keep the last batch or refugees from Earth? Didn't know they let anybody in."

"The refugees aren't 'kept' there, Pound. They stay of their own accord. And they'll be glad to see you. I used to know their captain pretty well. He's an old man by now but he might remember me. How about getting some of the boys together? We'll make a day of it tomorrow. Learn how our ancestors lived."

"Gee. Swell," cried Allison. "Anything to get out of this dump."

"Suits me," said Pound. "When do we start?"

* * * *

Merek briefed the party of two dozen or so who showed up the next morning. (The greater part of his men were still laid up.) "We're going to pay a visit to the descendants of the last persons to escape from Earth before it went nova. You'll find them a rather queer lot. But don't act surprised or laugh at their odd customs. They're very proud. Also, they're an independent nation with full diplomatic relations and all that.

"They drifted in here on a battered old hulk about a century ago. Since then they've flatly refused to becoming assimilated by making Bank deposits, using our servo-mechanisms or attending our schools. Out of respect for the past of the human race, the Council gave them a few thousand acres of land and has since left them strictly to their own devices."

"How many of them are there?" someone wanted to know.

"About a thousand men, women and children. And that's another thing I want to warn you about. You'll see great numbers of children and of more or less senile old people. This will be a new experience for you, but don't act surprised or shocked or we'll be shown the door. Understood? All right, let's start."

They completed their ten-mile hike well before noon. (Wheeled or winged vehicles were barred from the neighborhood of the reservation.)

They found themselves looking down from the brow of a wooded hill on a pleasant village made up of log houses. In its center was a square which served as final resting place for the wreckage of a space ship. There, too, the flag of the United Nations fluttered bravely from a tall pole.

Around the village lay a number of well-tended fields where men, women and older children were laboring with hand tools. Farther away, flocks of sheep, cows and horses were grazing.

"Don't they even use tractors?" Allison marveled.

"No," said Merek. "They will have nothing to do with power tools of any kind. The draft animals which they brought with them are used for the heaviest work, but everything else is done by manual labor. They contend that all machines, and especially all weapons, are enemies of the human race."

"But that kind of toil is fit only for robots," a sailor exploded.

"And when do they find time to think and study?" mused Pancrief. "Why, they're worse than the barbs. They've reverted to savagery."

"Don't be too sure," said Merek. "They're mighty nice folks."

A messenger had preceded the visitors, so they were met at the edge of the village by a round-eyed mob of overalled children of all ages. These showed no signs of timidity, or of rudeness either. They were neither hostile nor friendly.

The Centaurans formed ranks and marched smartly into the square. They were met at the flagpole by a bald and wrinkled ancient dressed in the frayed uniform of a U. N. Planetary Patrol Captain. He leaned heavily on the arm of a slight, sweetly rounded girl with freckles and red-gold hair. She wore no stockings and her knee-length dress was made of homespun.

"Welcome to our fair city, Admiral Merek," quavered the old man, "and another welcome to your crew. We have heard great things about your exploits."

"Thank you, Captain McCarthy," the Centauran replied with a salute. "Perhaps you remember me. I used to come here from Merekton frequently when I was a boy."

"Can't say I do. Can't say I don't. There are so many Mereks. They all look, think and dress alike." He chuckled, then became serious again. "This is my granddaughter, Sharon. She will show you about. You will, of course, be my guests for supper."

"Thank you, Captain. But we don't want to impose on your hospitality."

The graybeard straightened his back and frowned. "I insist, sir! As a duly appointed representative of the United Nations, I..." He shook his head as though to clear it. "No, that's not right any more."

"As ambassador..." Sharon prompted, looking embarrassedly at her toes.

"Ah yes. As a duly appointed ambassador to the Centauran Council… Oh, what nonsense am I talking? Our fare is rough—not fit for your palates…"

"You have wonderful food," Merek hastened to assure him as he seemed on the verge of senile tears. "Fried chicken. Baked beans. Pie. All the old dishes. My men and I will enjoy them immensely. We accept your invitation with pleasure."

"Heh. Heh. I believe I do remember you, boy. You're the little shaver who was always after me to tell you the old tales about John Paul Jones, and guerrilla fighting and how the Ark escaped from the Oligarchs. No wonder you gave the Siriuns such a licking out on—Arcon, wasn't it? How you could eat!"

"Grandpa!" Sharon spoke as to a child.

"And now, if you will excuse me," McCarthy said obediently, "I will leave you in Sharon's hands. I am an old man and mustn't stay too long under these alien suns." He tottered away with the girl's tender assistance and entered the largest of the cabins. The Centaurans shifted their feet and began to wish they had not come.

"He is the son of the original Captain McCarthy who brought the Ark in," Merek told them. "He has aged dreadfully since I knew him. Seems to be convinced that *he* made the trip, they tell me.

"Boy, I'm glad I don't have to get old, ever," Pound breathed.

"Oh, I don't know," Allison disagreed. "He seems to be having a pretty good time and he has a granddaughter to take care of him. Why, I'll bet *my* granddaddy has forgotten I'm alive."

To their growing surprise, the men all had a good time that day. They inspected the wreck of the Ark and marveled that such a rattletrap could have left Earth's atmosphere, let alone make a trip of more than four light years. They gradually made friends with the children. They went out into the weedless fields and found the people direct and sincere, even though they did have calloused hands and smelled of honest sweat and manure.

They couldn't keep their eyes off the laughing, bright-eyed girls they met. And, amazingly enough, they were completely taken by the old people who sat, gnarled hands folded, in their doorways or under the trees in the square, and told them long, rambling tales of Earth's proud history and its last tragic, flame-whipped years.

Pancrief, particularly, seemed hypnotized by Sharon. He followed her about like a dog, laughed at her simple jokes and looked at her until she blushed and stammered but did not take offense. She was so utterly naive and so different from any girl he had ever met that the cynical Pizarian fell head over heels in love at first sight. Once Merek saw him surreptitiously take out of his wallet the photograph of the Pizarian girl whose name he had forgotten and tear it into small bits.

"Are all those things true that the old folks have been telling us, sir?" Pound asked Merek that evening when they were seated at long trestle tables in the square, attacking the strange and delicious foods with which the women of the colony kept heaping their plates. "About Christopher Columbus crossing the Atlantic Ocean in a rowboat, I mean, and how that fellow Drake sank the French Armada? I don't remember learning stuff like that in school."

"They have mixed things up a trifle, but you'll find even more exciting true tales like those in the old printed books if you take the trouble to read them."

"Makes you sort of proud to be human, doesn't it?" said the lieutenant as he investigated a piece of pie. "Guess that's what makes these poor folks keep their chins up."

Merek was doing some deep thinking. He felt that the answer to the barbarian onslaught was almost within his grasp. As the men marched home through the starlight, singing the quaint folksongs they had learned after supper, he kept turning the problem over in his mind. Somehow, he must make all Centaurans proud that they were men—proud enough to fight for their heritage. But how? Send the ancient minstrels of the reservation throughout the planets? In three months? Ridiculous! Besides, Mercon, Arcon and Pizar had proud histories of their own, though they were almost unknown except to savants. His head began to ache again.

As the weary days rolled by, the grounded admiral began making frequent trips to Mercon City. He told himself he went to see Iskra, who was still in a hospital bed, weak and helpless as a kitten. He told himself he went to seek solutions to his insoluble problem in the endless stacks of the Council library. He told himself he went to escape his well-meaning but boring relatives. He would not admit that his long talks with Marian in her quiet office had anything to do with the matter.

Yet, like everyone else who had met her, he had fallen completely under the secretary's spell. Her remote beauty, which seemed the product of some alien star, held him breathless. The clean fragrance of her body made his senses reel. Her mind, crammed with the knowledge of ages, made him want to grovel at her naked feet.

With a motherly interest which he sometimes vaguely resented, she taught him to use the film-and-dot library indices which made the recorded history of the three planets almost instantly available.

In the dust-covered metal foil books and the later tri-di films he learned the full details of how his forebears fought out from Earth toward the rim of the galaxy along the only route not barred to them by the lordly Siriuns.

He saw them besieged at their first base on Pizar by the semi-intelligent primates which were dominant there; saw the mad suicide charge led by young Mendez which broke the strangling ring about the camp.

He watched them expand to Mercon and Arcon as the old guard of First Generationers died one by one. He learned how Franklin and a few surviving comrades created the Memory Bank so their sons and daughters could live longer than their allotted "three score and ten" and thereby acquire the maturity needed to lift the race above the Cain and Abel thinking which had always shackled it.

Then, abruptly, the epic story ended. It was succeeded by recordings of a placid, almost changeless flow of life on fully developed, rich and peaceful planets. He turned from the screen, baffled and saddened.

"The sap went out of our people centuries ago," he muttered.

"I know." Marian pressed his hand. "The Memory Bank was a magnificent try, but it failed. It prolonged life, but it stopped progress."

"Why?" he cried. "Granted that, in order to continue living indefinitely, wise men must deposit parts of their wisdom in the Bank as the decades pass, we were always told that that wisdom had merely been transferred to imperishable electronic records, and was available for study and synthesis. Surely the accumulated knowledge of a millennium can produce some philosophy, or some weapon, which can defeat the barbarians."

"Have you ever listened to a Bank deposit?" she asked with infinite sorrow.

"Never. They are restricted to savants, I was always told."

"No longer to you. We have the deposits of all Councilors available here at the Capitol. You may listen to one of Franklin's, if you wish."

She led him to a chair in the corner of the room. Lifting a complicated, helmet-like affair out of a niche in the wall, she adjusted it on his temples and flipped a switch...

An alarm was shrilling. He stretched out a cramped arm and shut it off. Why, he thought, can't I ever remember to get one of those ionization gadgets which would wake me gently at just the right moment?... This dark brown taste...shouldn't smoke cigarettes after dinner at my age! Franklin's still a child when it comes to appeasing his appetites... How old am I anyway? Let's see...this is May first, 2981, A.D... Now whatever does "A.D." mean?... Oh yes, "Anno Domini... Christians to the lions... Cold in this room! Or is my circulation acting up again?... Where are those slippers?... Confound that lazy robot...getting old along with me, perhaps... Where is the damned tooth polish? Maybe it would help to get my eyes open and look for it!... Ah! Refreshing. No wonder they advertise it so heavily, although the sight of a man cleaning his teeth is not particularly edifying. Now let's see. What's up today?... Conference with that fool,

Poynetz… He hasn't had a new thought since the pigs ate grandpa…has style though!… People's choice… Young squirt! He can't be over three hundred… Wonder why they went for grandpa… Bacon!… Oh yes, bacon and eggs… Traditional American breakfast food… Pigs all died here… Grandpas all lived… Still have eggs, anyway, though they don't seem to taste as good as they used to… Now where did that confounded, idiotic robot put my new robe?… Servo-mechanism! Hah!

There was a distant click. Merek found himself staring dazedly at Marian.

"Had enough?" she asked.

"You mean…" He leaped to his feet. "That's the kind of junk the Bank vaults are stuffed with?"

"Franklin's is high-order material. Remember, he is a genius. Some of the deposits are—horrible." Her eyes were bitter.

"How long was I…listening?"

"About a minute."

"During which time a genius crawled out of bed, put on his slippers and washed his teeth. Ten minutes, let's say. It's complete recall, isn't it?" As she nodded, he rushed on: "Then, to listen to a full ten-year deposit, one would have to withstand about a year of that drivel in the hope of locating a worthwhile thought or two?"

"That's right. In the brain, recollections like those on which you eavesdropped are brought to consciousness rarely, if ever. You must understand that the brain has an indexing system infinitely superior to the film-and-dot system used by our libraries. That index can sort a needed memory out of a million unwanted ones and bring it to consciousness almost instantly."

"And the Bank has no index?" he gasped.

"All it has is the name of each depositor and a chronology."

"Impossible."

"Merek, it has been my life task to develop a workable index. For almost a thousand years I have spent most of my waking hours trying to solve the riddle. I have failed!" She bowed her splendid head.

"But why? It seems simple."

"To a layman perhaps… Come, let us sit down… The Bank," she continued in her best lecturing style when they had made themselves comfortable, "is merely Franklin's further development of work started back in 1950 by a Doctor Goldman of Syracuse University. Goldman discovered that radar could be used to pick up and put on a moving map the tiny electrical impulses and accompanying activities of the brain. It was but a short step to the analysis of such impulses by means of the cybernetic calculators then coming into use.

"Franklin and his associated surgeons took the next step when they determined that senility is caused by the fact that the brain's own index has its limitations. That is, the number of brain molecules upon which memories can be impressed seem almost infinite, but the synaptic 'connectors' are much fewer."

"You mean," Merek floundered, "that the brain's 'switchboard' finally becomes so overloaded that calls for needed memories get lost in the shuffle?"

"Something like that," Marian condescended. "Franklin reasoned that if he could wipe the memory impressions off a part of the brain molecules which serve as nature's own memory bank, not only would he relieve congestion in the synaptic 'switchboard,' but the cleaned molecules could be re-used to store more up-to-date knowledge."

"I see." The admiral clutched at another analogy. "Too much alcohol will produce amnesia by wiping impressions off the cortex—although the molecules seldom are good for much afterward."

"True. Franklin's technique did not damage the brain. It merely removed a decade of impressions, beginning with those of infancy and early youth, and continuing so that the brain of the depositor never retained more than ninety years of its knowledge. Then he made the final step by transferring those impressions on an electronic brain. Theoretically, they remained available for reference at any time."

"But practically," said Merek, "he only recorded the thoughts of depositors, both inconsequential and important, in chronological order. To find any information of value, one would have to wade through the entire hodgepodge. I'd go crazy!"

"Most investigators would, and did, until the deposits became so extensive that we practically gave up attempting to scan them."

"You mean they're not used any more?" He thought with horror of the millions of deposit panels in the Bank vaults of three planets, each bearing on its face the name and reference number of a depositor, and a date.

"Very seldom, unless where some specific piece of information which is hinted at, pretty definitely pinpointed as to date, but not fully explained in the printed and tri-di library records. Then we dig into them. Of course, we could bring the original depositor back to the Bank, temporarily yank out a later hunk of his memory, substitute the old one we wanted to scan and let him use his own index, which he still retains, to find what we're after. That's quick and certain but it causes psychological and physiological shock. Repeated too often, it leads to the madness or death of the depositor."

"There's no other way?" He felt sick.

"Oh," she shrugged, "it is possible to set the deposit record just at the level of consciousness of the investigator and let him listen while doing other work. That technique suppresses the inconsequential stream-of-consciousness stuff but allows the peaks—when the brain is doing constructive thinking—to attract the attention of the scanner. I've used that method in an emergency, but I've had to take a long rest afterward to avoid a nervous breakdown."

"Then the interest paid on depositors…?"

"Just a fiction to insure prompt deposits and keep depositors happy."

"So the Bank is completely useless."

"It has kept people from dying," she said quietly. "Also I think, though I can't prove it, that it has gradually enlarged Centauran brain capacity. Our memories go back only a century, but our retentiveness may extend over a millennium. Even though I, for example, do not actually remember nine-tenths of the experiences I have had, the skills and other things I have forgotten may continue to mould my thinking and my unconscious acts. And, of course, there's always the faint possibility that I may be able to invent an index for the Bank. That would throw open all the knowledge of a thousand years to us. Surely then, we could find a way of stopping those awful troglodytes from Omega."

"Can you find an index in three months, Marian?" For once he pitied her, as she bowed her head and two tears dropped on her folded hands.

"I have an idea," he said at last. "Let me try. I have a fresh viewpoint. Oh no, not the index. That is beyond my powers. But perhaps I might hit on a method for building some sort of radiation screen. Once we had that, we could hold off the barbs indefinitely. We could throw it around our ships or our cities…"

"A radiation *screen*?" Her eyes brightened at this challenge. "That is a contradiction in terms, Merek. It's like speaking of a 'black white.'"

"Perhaps a black white would be a gray," he argued. "It's worth trying."

"It has been tried," she shrugged. "For hundreds of years by our best minds."

"I have another idea," he grinned.

"Yes?" She leaned toward him, unconsciously tempting.

"Let's order a bottle of Scopio, some soda and ice, and have several stiff drinks."

"Scopio?" she frowned. "Oh no. Alcohol dulls my thinking. Although," she touched a button, "there's no reason why you shouldn't have a drink."

CHAPTER XII

Weeks of heartbreaking work followed, but Merek's screen and Marian's index remained as unattainable as ever. Both the admiral and the secretary grew thin and wan, but they refused to give up, although the odds against them were millions to one.

Then, when Merek was at the breaking point, he received a call from the hospital. Iskra, he was told, was well enough to be taken to his home to convalesce.

She was only a shell of her former self, he found, drawn, pale, antiseptically clean for the first time, and bitter because the doctors had told her that her right arm probably would remain stiff for the rest of her life.

Iskra took a faint interest when he took her sightseeing in Mercon City. She viewed it from the same vantage point as that of a butcher examining the carcass of a fat steer. But Merekton left her cold.

"Merek folk like ghost," she complained after a day or two of it. "Iskra 'ear mind go 'blah, blah, blah,' roun' an' roun'. Walk roun' dead."

"Me too?"

"Oh no." She patted his hand. "Merek mind go 'Zit. Zit. Zit,' like sword dat miss." And then she reminded him of her telepathic powers by adding: "Lis'en too much to ol' book. Talk too much, mebbe so, to Marian."

"Oh." He turned red under her steady gaze.

"Dat aw ri'." She looked away quickly. "Marian plenty smart, like Merek. Iskra no goo' now. Arm stiff. No fight any mo'."

"Nonsense," he tried to laugh. "Come on over to the rest home. The boys are dying to see you."

She cheered up at the rousing reception she received from the sailors, all of whom were on their feet now and chafing at their enforced inaction. After that she spent most of her waking hours with them, avoiding Merek except at mealtime. As she became strong, she also made many visits to the reservation with the sailors. Like them, she seemed far more at home with the refugees than she did with any member of the Merek clan except young Matilda.

"Whatever do you see in that creature?" said Merek's mother one day. "She scandalizes the family by running around in that awful kilt. And yesterday I caught her out in the kitchen, eating with her *fingers*!"

"Oh, Mother," said Matilda crossly. "She's really awfully nice. And she can read your mind, so you'd better not even think things like that."

"Iskra's a splendid young animal, of course," said Merek, senior, who had an eye for the ladies, "but not your type, son. Not your type at all."

Whereupon Merek found it necessary to make another hurried trip to the Capitol.

On his final visit, Marian forgot her principles and had one drink with him.

"Nothing can be done," she said as she traced geometric designs with a slim gold fingertip in the dew on her glass.

"Nothing," he answered glumly. "Today I wandered through the city, talking to passers-by. There's no heart in them. They won't fight with our present set-up. And, even if we did find the screen or the index now, there's no time to use them. The truce has only a month more to run."

"I had a dream last night," she said. "Death came into this room in a black robe, asking a ransom for Mercon. You seized him by the throat. He flapped about like a big bird, snapping his teeth at you. Finally you let him go. You couldn't choke him… Death doesn't breathe." She shuddered, finished her drink and added: "Franklin wants you to stand by with the *Alpha* to take him to Omega to sign our formal surrender."

"Let Mendez do it. I will not go."

"Why?" The word was a whisper.

"He always has been an ambassador to other systems, hasn't he?"

"Yes." Marian made circles on the table top with the wet bottom of her glass. "Mendez made our very first treaty, with the Siriuns. Later he reestablished contact with the barbarians and opened up Omega for trade—worse luck."

"What's the real truth behind that Siriun treaty?" Merek poured another drink. "History says it was a great thing for us."

"It was a face-saving compromise." Her voice was bitter. "The Siriuns caused us a great deal of trouble in the first half millennium, you know. Their ships tried to turn us back when we were halfway out from Earth."

"I never could understand how we held out against those invisible devils."

"The old *Tellus*, which we captured from the oligarchs, was an interplanetary liner which our technicians converted for deep space travel. She was armed only with mines and short-range cannon. The Siriun ships which intercepted her seemed no better armed but they confused our pilots by some sort of telepathic broadcasting.

"Franklin dreamed up a counter weapon, put it in a lifeboat and went out on a suicide mission. The boat was shot to pieces. Franklin was the only crew member rescued but he was badly wounded. When he recovered he could not remember how the weapon had been made. I have gone over his first deposit many times. When it reaches that point the recording blanks out. Strange…"

"Yet the weapon must have been potent," said Merek. "The Siriuns kept their distance after that."

"Yes, for a time," she agreed. "The *Tellus* reached Pizar; later we colonized all the Centauran planets. But whenever we tried to expand beyond this system, the Siriuns managed to block us.

"When the barbarians finally broke through from dying Earth, the situation became tense again. The Siriuns had learned to tolerate us but they seemed to be in deadly fear of the barbs. Wanted them exterminated."

"Perhaps," said Merek thoughtfully, "it was because the atomic radiations of the endless Terran war had mutated the barbs until they were on the verge of using telepathy, not like an uncertain toy as we Centaurans do, but as a weapon like the Siriuns do."

"Perhaps." She held out her glass absent-mindedly. "Although how those creatures…"

"That reminds me," he interrupted. "Why aren't the refugees telepathic? They stayed on Earth until only a few months before the final blowup."

"The refugees kill all mutations at birth."

"Those gentle people?" Merek thought of Captain McCarthy and his sweet daughter.

"It's part of their religion, philosophy, or whatever you call it. They consider it no sin to do away with changelings—to preserve the old ways."

"Hmmm. But we were talking of the first Siriun treaty."

"Oh yes. Well, in the early days Centauran ships made repeated attempts to investigate the Dark Planet. They never returned… No, one did manage to get back with half its crew turned gibbering idiots. The pilot told a wild yarn about losing his way.

"Anyway, when we welcomed the barbarians, the Siriuns sent orders for one of our ships to come to their hideout and negotiate a treaty. Mendez volunteered for the mission. He came back with the treaty, such as it was. But when we tried to find out what had happened out there, his mind—and his deposit, too—were complete, jittery blanks, just like Franklin's. Even after this last trip out—the one you were on—he came back on the verge of a complete breakdown, the Bank reports."

"I know." Merek was trying desperately to think his way through this maze of contradictions. "But that treaty: What were its provisions?"

"We were to limit the populations of the three planets, stop trying to colonize other systems and expel the barbarians. In return, the Siriuns would leave us in peace and trade with us. Come to think of it"—Marian looked at him oddly—"the Centauran doldrums might be said to date from that treaty."

"You can't have progress and maintain the *status quo* at the same time," Merek shrugged. "Well, it's only fair to let Mendez finish what he started by taking Franklin to Omega." He hesitated and then rushed on: "With your permission, Intelligence, I want to leave this system before the barbs come. There's really nothing more I can do here. And my men fought too well and are too loyal to become slaves. We may be able to found a colony on some distant planet."

"That doesn't sound like you." She finished her drink and made a face over it.

"I know," he said miserably. "But can you suggest an alternative?"

Marian stared at her toes for a while, then shook her bright head.

"Why don't you come with us?"

"Oh no!" She kept her eyes lowered. "My duty is here."

"What duty? This civilization is dying. Your duty is to help build another."

She rose and paced the room, studying the hundred panels of her calculators as though seeking an answer among their inscrutable tubes.

"What about that barbarian wench?" she astounded him by saying at last.

"I-Iskra?" He hated himself for stammering. "What has she to do...why, we're just blood brothers—I mean, we saved each other's lives. That's all."

"All, Merek?"

"Confound it!" He jumped up and gripped her smooth shoulders to stop that eternal pacing. "Iskra is not quite human. Mutation, you know. Let me..."

"Human enough!" Marian's firm chin went up. "You just want to use my brain in starting your colony." Tears formed and she dashed them away. "Oh, why did I drink that awful Scopio? I'm all confused. But I think"—she threw back her head—"that you should bring this—Asta, is that her name?—here to see me before we discuss this matter farther. You may go now!"

* * * *

Merek approached the meeting between the two women with fear such as he had never felt when facing barbarian guns. He scrubbed Iskra until her bronzed hide turned pink. He brushed the tangles out of her curls while she fidgeted and swore. He even enticed her to use some of the perfume which was fashionable that year. But when he brought one of Matilda's loveliest gowns she flatly refused to put it on, although she fingered the shining fabric wistfully.

"Iskra warrior. Wear kilt!" she said flatly.

"At least let me have the damned thing cleaned."

"Aw ri'!" She hurled the moth-eaten excuse for a garment at him. He thought he heard her giggle as the door irised shut behind him.

He expected an explosion when his "blood brudder" strutted into Marian's office without touching fingers to forehead, as was the Centauran custom. The secretary turned white but said nothing.

Clumsily—her arm hung stiffly—the battle-scarred veteran hitched herself to the top of Marian's desk, swung her heels and fished in her pockets.

"Marian 'ave gum?" She proffered a battered stick.

Merek held his breath.

"Thank you, my good girl." The Secretary accepted the peace offering but did not unwrap it. "I suppose Admiral Merek has told you he intended to emigrate."

"Yah." Iskra nodded. "Merek big foo'."

"And has he told you he wants me to go with him?" If Marian had been a cat she would have licked her chops at this point.

"Yah. Dat aw ri'." She blinked her eyes in an unwarriorlike manner. "Iskra no goo'. Sword arm stiff." She demonstrated.

"I didn't mean it that way." Marian's face turned scarlet.

"Mind mean it."

"Why am I a fool for wanting to leave?" Merek interposed.

"Jus' talk," she answered with a slow wink. "Merek no quit."

"But we can't win."

"No lick Rolphson," she agreed with pride. "Lick Siriun, mebbe so."

"How?" Marian leaned forward tensely. Although she abominated all barbarians and outwardly scorned them, she would not have remained Secretary had she really been so small as to ignore their telepathic and other gifts. "How, Asta?"

"Name Iskra. Sub-chief Rabbit Clan!" The girl's composure was ruffled.

"Excuse me, Chief Iskra." In her eagerness Marian was almost humble. "You mean, I suppose, that the inhabitants of Sirius' Dark Planet are the real enemies of both our peoples. But their civilization is so superior to ours that..."

"Hah!" Iskra spat on the shining floor.

"Well, isn't it?"

"Siriun know 'ow throw big scare. Dat aw. Franklin mos' lick Siriun once. Centauran 'elp. Barb 'elp. Refugee 'elp. Lick goo' dis ti'."

"How did you know about Franklin's weapon?" Marian was really shaken now.

"Read in mind."

"Do you know how the weapon was made?"

"No. But Bank know."

"It doesn't," Marian sighed. "I've searched the deposits. They go blank when I reach that period. The bank actually jitters. Acts as if it had had a nervous breakdown." She was treating the barbarian as an equal.

"No matter." Iskra shrugged her good shoulder. "Bank show Centauran 'ow be brave...fight goo'."

"How could the Bank show people how to be brave, child?"

"No child! Big girl!"

"All right. All right," Merek cut in. "If you have any ideas, explain them."

"'Ard say in silly word," she frowned. "Wait... Iskra try talk big, like Centauran. Den mebbe so Marian, Merek understan'." Her eyes slitted in concentration. Eventually she resumed in halting but almost perfect English:

"Ol' book—the old books that Rolph read talked a great deal about the 'dead hand of the past.' They said too much reliance on tradition makes people rigid and conservative so they do not change and grow. On the other hand, there are people like you Centaurans who despise tradition and have no real interest in their past. They become decadent and weak. But, the books said, there is also a 'living hand of the past'; the great memories which make men proud to be men; willing to fight to the death rather than become slaves. The barbarians—and the refugees—pass along those great memories from generation to generation in stories and folksongs. But the Centaurans..."

"Just stuff them in the Bank and forget them," Marian agreed. "But what is the alternative? No human brain can encompass a thousand years of memories."

"No need to." Iskra was growing impatient. "Just keep the high spots. Leave all the rest in the Bank but give back to their owners the proud thoughts—the ones that make men fight for liberty."

"Impossible!" Marian pressed a hand to her lips. "And yet..." She began pacing like her old dynamic self. "We'll use an electronic relay to screen out or suppress the drivel. We'll return what is left to the Depositors. Mendez will forget he bought a new uniform three months ago. But he'll remember how *and why* he led that suicide charge against the aborigines 900 years ago... Oh, wonderful! We'll be like gods. Here!" She snatched a plascript pad and wrote equations like mad. "This should do it... How stupid we have been."

"Still stupid," said Iskra, looking over the secretary's shoulder and dropping back into patois to express her disgust. "No work *dat* way."

"Of course it will!" Imperious once more, now that she had a lead, Marian brushed the objection aside. "You and Merek run along like good children and let me work this out."

Merek ventured a protest. He might have been speaking to a deaf woman.

"Why do you think her approach won't work?" he asked after they had tiptoed out.

"Doctor no can cure self!" She shook her curls angrily.

"Why are you trying to help us?" he puzzled. "If Marian's plan does work, your people have no chance of invading the Centauran planets. Nothing will stand against us."

"Better barb no come 'ere," she answered slowly. "No ready live long ti' yet. Mus' stay Omega. Be 'appy dere if Dark no come 'gain."

"Ummm. And if it doesn't work?"

"Dark come Mercon, mebbe so." She shivered as she paced down the marble steps. "Iskra, Merek go 'ome now. Sit in sun."

"You don't think too much of Marian, do you?" he prodded.

"Sweet girl," she yawned. Then, with renewed eagerness as she pointed to a shining emporium across the grassy street: "Take Iskra to store. Buy pretty thing."

They returned to Merekton laden with purchases, mostly junk jewelry and other gewgaws with which Iskra delighted in decking her naked person to the scandal of all Mereks. Then, for several days, they loafed in the sun as she had suggested, swam under the trailing willows and paid a number of visits to the reservation.

Iskra had taken a tremendous liking to Sharon McCarthy and was doing everything in her power to forward Pancrief's romance. One of the ways in which she accomplished this was to engage in lengthy and sometimes bitter arguments with Captain McCarthy over the merits and demerits of non-resistance, thereby giving Sharon and the lean Pizarian a chance to wander off, hand-in-hand.

"Must resist evil," was the nub of her argument which the old man could not quite dodge. "Must fight evil to death."

"But people are not evil," he would plead as they foregathered with Merek under the trees on the square while scores of old folk and children gathered 'round to listen and sometimes to inject arguments of their own.

"Neither are machines," she would counter. (She never used verbal shorthand when talking to the completely non-telepathic refugees.) "So why fight machines. They are only tools made by people whom you say are good."

"Evil thoughts destroyed Earth," Iskra would insist. "Good Earth people fought other good Earth people. They never bothered to stamp out the thoughts that made good people hate each other—or to wonder where those thoughts came from."

"You barbarians just like to fight for the fun of it," the captain might snarl at this point. Or he might fly into a senile rage if Sharon happened to be nearby and said: "There's something to Iskra's argument, Father. Non-resistance didn't save Earth."

"Only a few thousand of us refugees-to-be tried it," he would thunder.

"And where are we now? Living on a reservation like the Indians used to. That is not life."

Whereupon the captain would stomp off to his cabin in a pet and his daughter would take his place.

"There *are* evil people, I think," she ventured once while the onlook-ers shook their heads in silent reproof. "Evil people are those who think all other people are evil."

"That doesn't make sense, Sharon," Pancrief objected. "You are defin-ing evil in terms of itself."

"I'm just a girl," she answered, "but I have talked a great deal with Father, who is foolish only when he gets to feeling old. Once he told me there are just two classes of people: Those who hold that men, with a few shining exceptions, are all evil, and those who believe that men, with a few shameful exceptions, are pretty decent.

"I'll go a step farther. I'll agree with Iskra to this extent: The few evil men should be fought, conquered and put somewhere where they cannot corrupt good men." She sprang to her feet. "I must see that Father gets un-dressed and to bed." Extending a hand to Iskra, she added, "Come again, please. I like you barbarians better than the Merconians. I can understand you."

"What about Pizarians?" Pancrief asked.

"Oh, you are barbarous enough so I can understand about half of what you say."

"Which half?"

"The half in which you make love to me," she whispered in his ear before she ran after her father.

"Sharon smart," Iskra said as they walked back to Merekton under the stars. "Refugee no stay on reservation if Sharon chief."

"You said once the refugees might be able to help us against Siriun," Merek recalled. "How could they do that?"

"Barbarian telepath," she answered slowly. "Siriun better telepath. Twist barb mind in knot. Killum, even. Centauran telepath li'l bit. Siriun no kill Centauran. Jus' mix up thought. Makeum weak—like back on Earth, mebbe so."

"You mean," shouted Merek, "that it may have been Siriun tinkering with our minds which caused the final wars back home?"

"W'y not?" she shrugged. "Mebbe dat w'y refugee keep mind shut.

Kill mutation. Stay sane dat way. Siriun no can touch."

"So, if the refugees could get over their phobia against machinery they could pilot a ship right to the Dark Planet instead of going to pieces the way any of us would if we tried to go there without permission?" This from Pancrief.

"Yah. Refugee come Mercon in ship."

"Fact is," said Merek, "they almost worship that old wreck on the common despite their hatred of other machines. Look into this, Pan. Iskra has something."

The admiral forgot all about that conversation when he reached home. Waiting for him was a message from Marian which read:

"Demonstrating suppressor to Council tomorrow at 800. Attend with Iskra."

CHAPTER XIII

After some trouble about passes they entered the heavily-guarded Council Chamber. On hospital beds in front of the platinum rail lay four still figures, their heads encircled by encephalographic helmets of a new and complicated design. Cables ran from each helmet to an outlet connecting it with the proper Memory Bank channel. A doctor and two armed guards watched over the sleepers.

Merek saw, with a sort of horror, that Marian occupied the first bed. She looked small and somehow unfinished, because the helmet hid her hair and part of her face. His amazement grew when he realized that the second cot was filled by Mendez's hulking form. Cots three and four held a man and a woman he did not know.

Seated under the ever-changing mural, the Council members leaned forward tensely, listening to President Franklin. He evidently had been speaking in camera for some time.

"To sum up," the young-old man was saying, "Her Intelligence perfected a suppressor relay that responds to every thought of a Bank depositor—withdrawer would be a more accurate word in this case. Any ah, client must recently have made his routine ten-year deposit. As a result, one-tenth of his brain cells have been wiped clean, ready to receive impressions, either new or old.

"The new helmet is placed on his head. His own deposits, beginning with the earliest years of his life and ending with the latest, are played into the blank section of his brain from the panels where they previously had been placed for safekeeping. Thus he reviews his past experiences, beginning with his first memories as an infant or even those in the months between conception and birth.

"But since, under Marian's new system, the withdrawer is fully conscious and in control of the suppressor relay, he need no longer overload his cortex by reliving every moment of his past life. He lets the 'clutch' of the recording slip, as Her Intelligence explained it to me, until it brings to light some event which profoundly affected his development. He re-impresses this incident on his mind, lets the record race until another peak is reached, records again and so continues until he has regained all the key recollections of his lifetime."

"How long does the process require," asked Poynetz, the sour-faced philosopher, "and why was the full council not consulted before its Secretary was allowed to participate in this…dubious experiment?"

"The entire re-recording requires 12 hours or less depending upon the age of the client and therefore the mass of material to be scanned," Franklin answered. "The experiment, as you call it, was begun yesterday. In view of the emergency which has arisen, there was no chance to assemble the Council beforehand."

"You mean the new ultimatum from Rolphson?" Councilor Anthony of Arcon inquired.

"Exactly. The new emperor suspects there is something in the wind. He warns us his fleet will attack unless we surrender within the week. It was under those circumstances that Admiral Mendez volunteered to undergo treatment. He hopes it will enable him to remember long-forgotten campaigns and strategies. Our fleet is ready to depart at once if the—experiment—is successful."

"And Marian?" someone asked.

"I know." Franklin bowed his head. "If anything goes wrong we may be in serious trouble without her great wisdom. I tried to argue her out of being first to test the suppressor. She insisted. I had no power to forbid her."

"And the other two—victims?" That was Poynetz again.

"They are an average citizen and his wife who volunteered to act as controls."

"Your Intelligences!" cried the doctor. "Admiral Mendez is rousing."

Mendez yawned, stretched, waited calmly for the helmet to be removed, sat up and scratched his barrel chest.

"Wonderful! Wonderful!" He saluted the Council. "A revelation. Remember every worthwhile incident in my entire naval career. Now let the barbs try anything!" His hooded eyes, clear as those of a young hawk, stared through Merek for a long moment. Without returning the other's salute Mendez bent over Marian, who was beginning to stir.

The Secretary rose briskly as soon as the helmet was off.

"I know how to build my Bank index now," she said. "Have the main calculator cleared! I begin work at once. The index must be built on Beacon or one of Arcon's moons because of its tremendous size." She faced the Council imperiously. "Drop all other work. This matter will require your undivided attention for the next five years." Suddenly she wavered and grasped the rail for support. "Need all the calculators," she mumbled. "Five thousand technicians. I…" She passed a hand over her face in the old uncertain gesture.

"Marian!" Merek shook her gently. "Wake up."

"Who are you, sir?" The words flicked like a lash as she recovered herself.

"Merek," he stammered as those great eyes studied him without recognition. "Admiral Merek."

"Nonsense. Admiral Mendez commands the Centauran fleet. What have you done with my husband?"

"Here I am, dear." Mendez slipped his arm around her rigid shoulders. To the astounded Council he added, "Don't worry. She'll be all right in a few hours. Quite a shock, you know. Let me handle her." He started leading her from the room.

"Merek stop Mendez!" Iskra gasped. "Mendez aw bad now! Quick!"

Merek pushed forward. An overly-officious guard barred his way. Before he could be placed, the admiral was at the door. Merek started to follow but Franklin, not understanding what was going on, hammered with his gavel.

"Admiral Merek," he thundered. "The Council has not dismissed you."

Merek gave it up. Placing his wrist communicator to his lips he called Pancrief on their private channel.

"Get the crew to battle stations," he commanded when the other came in. "Take the *Terra* up a mile or so and stand by for orders—*my* orders. Trouble's brewing here, I think. Over."

"Roger. Have fun," came the answer.

The last two sleepers were sitting up now. The woman spoke first:

"Married to a nincompoop!" she hissed as she stared across the beds at her weak-chinned, blinking husband. "I, who was once the toast of Mercon… I, who thrilled millions with my dancing in the early days… I, who have had a planetary governor as a lover and a Councilor as a husband… To have sunk so low. Oh, shame. Shame!" Sobbing wildly, she ran out of the room.

"What a fool I have been, Your Intelligences," the man said when she had gone. "For almost a thousand years I have been running frantically about, seeking new sensations, experiences, adventures, women, wealth, beauty and excitement. I have neglected every worthwhile pursuit to do these senseless things because, never until now have I known enough to realize that, all the time…what I really sought was—this!"

Swift as a snake, he snatched an automatic from the holster of a nearby guard, placed the muzzle to his temple and pressed the trigger.

"Now," sneered Poynetz when the dead man had been carried out and the hubbub had subsided, "perhaps our Honorable President can explain this debacle."

"Theoretically…" Franklin ran his fingers through snowy hair. "Theoretically, the suppressor relay should have worked. I checked all of Marian's equations and plans. I have no idea what went wrong. Can anyone hazard a guess?"

"Iskra can." She strode forward nonchalantly, hands deep in the pockets of her kilt. She perched herself on the platinum rail, hooked bare toes around its graceful supports and rummaged for gum.

"Is this the barbarian you captured, Admiral Merek?" Franklin demanded.

"More or less. It would be wise to listen to her, Your Intelligence."

"Suppressor work fine," Iskra grinned at them. "Centauran mind no work."

"What's this all about?" shouted a Councilor.

"Iskra blood brudder to Merek," she began explaining, as though to a group of children. "Try be friend aw Centauran. Tell Marian if Centauran get pride back an' 'member 'ow fight, can make alliance wit' Rolphson. Lick Siriun."

"So she practically told Marian how to make the suppressor," Merek snapped. He had begun to suspect that Iskra was a fifth columnist, deliberately bent on Centauran defeat. "And look what happened."

"Marian no let Iskra say one thing." She looked at him sadly as she read his thoughts. "No goo' 'ave relay on suppressor worked by withdrawer from Bank. If withdrawer well-rounded person, come back, mebbe so, wit' big, well-rounded memory. But if one-track like Marian, 'oo spend thousand year hunt Bank index, come back, think only of index. If vain woman, 'member only vain thing. If 'ave suicide complex, understand. Shoot self quick."

"And if the withdrawer should be Mendez"—Merek choked on the developing thought—"with an overwhelming ambition, a thousand years of military experience, and a passionate craving for Marian..."

"Yah!" Iskra chewed her gum thoughtfully, eyes on some faraway scene. "Den Mendez think Centauran done fo'. Kidnap Marian. Go spaceport. Take up fleet. Go join Rolphson!"

Pandemonium broke loose in the chamber. Communicator screens flared to confirm the fact that the fleet already was taking the air. Orders were shouted, to be immediately countermanded. Attendants and guards ran hither and yon like rabbits. A number of august Councilors caught the infection and fled, white robes flapping. A world was ending!

Eventually only Franklin and Poynetz sat huddled on the dais amidst a shambles of overturned and broken chairs, facing Iskra and Merek outside the railing.

"I suppose," the philosopher gritted as he switched off the useless communicator, "that this woman should be arrested as a saboteur."

"Iskra try tell Franklin w'en Mendez leave wit' Marian."

"Yes. Yes. That's true," the president admitted and added pathetically: "Perhaps you will intervene for us with Rolphson when he lands."

"No goo'," she answered calmly. "If Rolphson land, Siriun send Dark. Make barb, Centauran go mad. Kill. Kill till none left. Den Dark Planet rule galaxy."

"Then there is no hope," said Poynetz.

"One…two…t'ree 'ope." She held up as many lean fingers. "Mebbe so fo'. Throw dice ri', still can win."

"How? How?" they clamored at her.

"One," she said, turning down a finger, "Merek 'ave ship wit' super-drive in air. Two." She repeated the gesture. "Ship can get to Beacon 'fore Mendez. Make alliance wit' Rolphson. T'ree. 'Ave refugee. Siriun no can 'urt 'em. Mebbe so guide barb fleet to Dark Planet. Fo'. Still can make Bank give back proud memory—tell 'ow Franklin almos' lick Siriun once."

"No time to try that again," said the president.

"Plenty ti'," she said firmly. "Iskra show." She hopped from her perch, picked up one of the headsets, stood a long moment as though listening, then, despite her stiff arm, began readjusting the wiring and relays with hands as deft as those of a technician.

"Dere," she said, presenting the helmet to Franklin. "Put on. Scan Bank deposits."

"Are you crazy, man?" Poynetz cried as the president made a motion as if to obey. "What do we know about this wretched girl? She is probably a spy. Don't touch that thing. It's a proven failure!"

"Poynetz," Iskra commanded. "Look at me." Reluctantly he did so. "Look in Iskra mind!" The philosopher's wizened face twisted into a knot as he fought to disobey. Then he sighed and relaxed.

Although Iskra's thoughts were directed at the philosopher, both Merek and Franklin sensed their general import. They were not brutal nor specific. They did not scratch the brain like rusty needles but soothed it like healing fingers.

"What are you? A superwoman?" Poynetz breathed at last.

"Girl!" she frowned. Then to Franklin: "Put on. No 'urt. No take long."

The president did her bidding and switched into his Bank channel.

Then something happened which Merek was never afterward able to describe properly. It was as though a clock or a tri-di film were being run backward. It was as though a butterfly were emerging from a cocoon. It was like Ponce de Leon sighting the fountain of youth. It was like all of those things and like none of them!

Outside the Capitol the sounds of mob hysteria began as the news of Mendez's defection leaked out. It mounted as the minutes and hours passed but inside the hushed chamber Iskra, Merek and Poynetz sat enthralled, watching the weariness of a thousand years pass from Franklin's face.

He did not become physically younger. His hair remained white and the wrinkles did not disappear. But, as time passed, his chin went up and his shoulders straightened. He breathed deeper. Color came into cheeks which had been like parchment. Instead of being an old, old man in a younger man's body, he became a young man in a body grown prematurely old.

Iskra watched the controls closely, with occasional glances at the big clock above the mural. At last she disconnected the helmet and put it aside.

"'Ow Franklin feel?" she asked.

"Fine!" He stood up and stretched until his muscles cracked. Then he frowned. "Who are you? What's going on here? And what room is this? I didn't know we had built anything so pretentious." He started as he caught sight of his fellow Councilor. "Ah, Poynetz! I thought you were out chasing aborigines."

"Uh... I..." Poynetz shot a look full of venom at Iskra.

"President Franklin," said the girl, looking steadily at the patriarch, "there is much to explain and little time to explain it... You understand the principle of the Memory Bank?"

"I had a hand in inventing it, young woman."

"When were the first units installed?"

"Any schoolgirl knows that—in 2075, the seventy-third year after our landing on Pizar."

"What year is this?"

"Why, 2081, of course."

"This is 3002, almost a thousand years after that landing."

"Nonsense." He was growing angry. "Who are you, anyway, wearing those outrageous clothes, or lack of them?"

She merely looked at him. His angry frown changed to one of puzzlement and, finally, of stunned acceptance.

"I believe you are telling the truth," he said at last. "But I am not sufficiently telepathic to read your thoughts clearly. Put them in words."

She outlined the situation: the collapse of Centauran morale and defense; the failure of Marian's suppressor; Mendez's defection; their desperate dream of striking at the Siriuns to cut the Gordian knot which was strangling humanity.

"To me, this is still the year 2081," Franklin groaned when she finished. "I am approaching my one hundredth birthday and preparing to make my first Bank deposit. The aborigines on Arcon are in revolt. We think Sirius is supplying them with arms... Poynetz..." He turned to his friendly enemy with outstretched hands. "Isn't—wasn't that the way things were?"

"I don't remember," stammered the philosopher. "My early memories are buried in score upon score of Bank panels."

"And my memories of later days?" Franklin asked.

"They, too, are deposited in the Bank," said Iskra. "You may study them later. Perhaps that is the proper use for Marian's suppressor. But now we want you to tell us what sort of weapon was employed against the Siriuns when you made that foray in the lifeboat."

"Oh—that!" The president's eyes closed in concentration. For perhaps five minutes he sat rigid. Then he sighed and shook his head. "I can't remember," he admitted bleakly. "It was—it was something which struck at some weakness we surmised the Siriuns had. There was no time to complete it on board the *Tellus*. She was beginning to slide off the route to Centaurus despite everything we could do. We loaded the pieces on the lifeboat and assembled them as we headed for the enemy fleet."

"Why didn't your boat slide off course too?" Merek asked.

"I don't know. Perhaps because the foray was organized on the spur of the moment, and the Siriuns were caught by surprise. Anyway, while I was bending over our weapon a rapidly rotating part of it broke. I was struck on the temple. Here…" He showed them the ancient scar just above his hairline. "When I regained consciousness I was in the hospital aboard the *Tellus*. They told me—but you know all that—that my companions must have got the weapon working after I was knocked out; that it must have thrown a scare into the Siriuns because they kept such a distance from us after that that their telepathing broadcasting was ineffective; that the lifeboat ran into a floating mine and was totally destroyed; that I must have been put in a space suit and cast adrift, possibly when the others saw that a collision was inevitable.

"Ever since," he concluded lamely, "I have tried to recall what that weapon was—and always I have failed. It is as though a dark curtain had fallen."

"Siriun devil trick." Iskra dropped back into the vernacular in her excitement. "Set up circular neuronic path in brain. Memory no los'. Jus' bury."

Poynetz was on his feet, shaking like a leaf. "Hypnotism!" he shouted. "Why did I never think of it? We must try to reach Franklin's unconscious!" He scrabbled in a satchel which a fleeing psychiatrist-councilor had left behind, came up with a gadget of bright lights and revolving mirrors.

"Wait," said Merek. "President Franklin has just been through a very trying experience. Do you think this is wise?"

"Now!" said Iskra. "Too late w'en Mendez join Rolphson."

"Shoot, Poynetz," said Franklin. "This is the first original idea you have had since the pigs ate Grandpa." He relaxed and stared into the spinning hypnotizer.

"Arthur Franklin," said the philosopher when the patriarch was asleep. "Can you hear me?"

"I hear you," came the toneless reply.

"Think back to the hour when your lifeboat left the *Tellus* to make contact with the Siriun navy. Tell me exactly what happened."

"Hank, Tom, Will and I are putting equipment aboard the boat," Franklin began in a muffled voice. "We have to act at once. The Siriuns have given the *Tellus* five hours to start decelerating or undergo what they call a mental bombardment of the first order. Hank thinks we can complete the weapon as we go out...

"We're aboard the boat now. It is expelled from its cradle. Tom is warming up the drive... We're moving toward the enemy fleet at the speed of the *Tellus* plus our own. Should make contact in twelve hours. Meantime, we have much work to do..." He lapsed into silence.

"Think forward to the time when you and the others are working over the weapon," Poynetz commanded. "Here's a plascript and stylus. Sketch the parts and circuits of your weapon."

Franklin's eyes remained closed but he took the stylus and began sketching.

"Can't show the completed machine yet," he said dreamily. "Hank designed the tuner. He's attaching it now. Looks like this." The stylus raced. "It revolves at tremendous speed... Hank is making the last connections on the printed circuit... Here...and here. His hands are shaking. This means life or death to all of us. Hank's lighting a cigarette before he flips the switch..."

"Ask him the purpose of the weapon," Merek whispered.

"Why, it's so simple I can't understand why we didn't think of it before," Franklin answered when the question had been relayed. "It's just an ultra-microwave transmitter which—wait!" His voice broke with excitement. "Hank has his nerves under control now. He's going to turn on the... Ohhhh!"

The president's voice rose to a scream of agony. He clapped both hands to his head, then toppled from his chair, unconscious. When Iskra and the others rushed to his aid they found blood oozing from that old wound on his left temple.

"My fault," mourned Poynetz. "I should have ask that question first."

"Can we revive him and try again?" Merek asked as he worked over the fallen man.

"I'm afraid not." Poynetz gnawed his lips. "There's a complete block. It would take weeks or months of treatment to break it down without killing him." He turned to Iskra. "Can you make out the purpose of the weapon he sketched?"

The girl shook her head.

"Could make machine," she said as she helped the others make Franklin as comfortable as possible on one of the cots. "Try out. See w'at 'appen.

Like 'aving weapon to kill fee but no know fee live."

"We know a little more than that," said Poynetz. "We know that, if it is tuned just so, it does something rough to Siriuns."

"I suggest you get several technicians to work on this, Your Intelligence," Merek proposed.

"If the techs haven't all run away." Poynetz pushed a button. Eventually a frightened little man scurried into the room, looked over the sketches, listened to their explanations, nodded his head doubtfully and scurried out with the plascript.

"I'm convinced the answer is just within our grasp," Merek raged as Poynetz pushed other buttons which brought a doctor and a nurse to attend Franklin. "All of these deposits available"—he swept an arm toward the shining panels ranged along one wall of the chamber—"and nothing comes out of them. Poynetz, you are the Council now. What do you suggest?"

"I think"—the philosopher placed his finger tips carefully together—"that the Bank—it was in quite a primitive state at that time, remember—must have received some sort of shock which blanked all its records for the period we are searching. Electronic brains, just like those of humans, are subject to nervous breakdowns when presented with insoluble problems or contradictory orders."

"Who could have given contradictory orders which would have sent the Bank into a tail spin?" Merek demanded.

"In those early days, in fact, up until the last few hundred years when the system became so complicated that authority had to be delegated to a Bank authority, the entire project was controlled by the Council," Poynetz answered.

"No one else?"

"Well, I seem to have read that during the period when the first treaty with Sirius was being negotiated and ratified Admiral Mendez was made an exofficio Council member."

"Mendez!" Merek grinned like a wolf. "Are his deposits available?"

Poynetz nodded to a series of gently glowing panels to the left of the dais.

Merek slapped one of Marian's new helmets on his head, adjusted the suppressor circuit, plugged it, on a hunch, into the panel bearing the numerals 2520-2530, and merged completely and at once with the mentality of his former superior officer. Merged, but was not submerged. He was still Merek listening to another's thoughts.

To his utter astonishment, he found that Mendez had a likeable mentality—vigorous, patriotic and with a healthy sense of humor—not in the least like the martinet he knew and despised.

At breakneck speed he skimmed through the events leading up to Mendez's departure for Sirius. They were all there, as crystal clear as though he were remembering events in his own life. In the admiral's stead, he paced the bridge of the big ship during takeoff from Mercon's space port. He skipped the endless months as the ship, which had no hyper drive, of course, drew nearer and nearer to the Dark Planet. He obeyed the sardonic telepathic instructions of his hosts to the letter as he lowered to a landing through 20 miles of dense fog. With Merek's lips, it seemed, Mendez gave orders for the opening of the main port...

And, after that order was issued, he remembered nothing more.

Oh yes, the relays on Mendez's panel—he could see them dimly as a sort of diaphanous background for the events he had been reliving—began flipping open and closed like mad. The mercury tubes of the circular memory channels danced with wavering lights. Eerie squeals, dregs of thoughts and supersonic whines filled his brain. But of what occurred after that port unscrewed he got not an inkling.

The next lucid, or semi-lucid, memory he could catch hold of showed him, still as Mendez, issuing orders to lift the ship for its return journey.

But the Mendez into whose brain he now peered was subtly different from the devil-may-care fighter who had landed on the Dark Planet. There was a mordant cynicism in that mind. There was overwhelming ambition. There was the pride of a Lucifer.

"From now on"—the concept formed in his mind like smoke seeping through damp leaves heaped on a roaring bonfire—"from now on I, Mendez, am the arbiter of..." The thought was cut off as though by a mental knife.

Merek made a motion as though to rip off the helmet. He was further from a solution than before. Then he hesitated. What had Poynetz said: "... The Bank must have received some sort of shock. Electronic brains, just like those of humans, are subject to nervous breakdowns."

And what do psychiatrists use to cure nervous breakdowns? Why they use shock—shock by electricity, drugs, even a hard slap in the face!

Waving away the questions which Poynetz and Iskra were shouting at him, Merek reset the dials; returned Mendez to the moment when he had landed in Siriun territory. Then, as memory started to black out, he seized a chair and began smashing at the glowing panel. When the chair broke apart he beat the thing with his fists and kicked it again and again. Shock indeed! He would give the damned machine a shock it would never forget!

Inside his head—Mendez's head—something exploded. Merek fell to his knees. A rusty needle was scratching at his brain. Agony such as he had never dreamed of coursed like acid through his psyche.

"No!" Mendez was screaming. "No!" In the pitch darkness he scrabbled vainly for the control button which would have sealed the ship and sent his men to battle stations.

"Too late," the needle incised his wincing cortex. "We are inside now. Our…superiors…will not let you escape." Other needles took up the attack. Hell opened.

"No!" panted Mendez. But this time he meant "Yes."

"That is better." The needle points withdrew ever so slightly. "Tell us. What was the weapon your people built on their little boat?"

"I don't know," the quivering husk of Mendez groaned. "Don't hurt me again."

"We won't hurt you. But we must alter you somewhat before we send you home with the treaty we have prepared. We must see that a small part of us remains always in your brain."

"No!" Aliened strained at the mental bonds which held him. "Not that. Not that."

"You won't be hurt, miserable worm," cooed the needles. "There! That didn't hurt a bit, did it? Now open wider!… There…and there! Perfect! A beautiful bit of surgery, isn't it, cousins?

"Forget now, Mendez. Stand up. Return to the bridge. Give the command for takeoff. Wrap your pink tentacles around this box. It contains the treaty. Ah, we're going to be good friends, aren't we all? We're going to establish the same control over Centaurus and Omega which we exercised over Earth, aren't we? And we're going to tear the Memory Bank apart to find the secret of Franklin's weapon or, failing that, to be sure that no human rediscovers it, aren't we, Mendez?"

The needles gave a final emphatic dig and withdrew.

Shaking as with the palsy, Merek tore the helmet from his head and hurled it into a far corner of the chamber.

"Jackpot!" he yelled crazily. "I hit the jackpot. Mendez has an incubus!"

He fainted.

CHAPTER XIV

Merek revived to find Iskra holding his head in her lap while Poynetz chafed his wrists. Franklin, a bandage around his head, was bending over them. In the background hovered the little tech.

"Took hours to bring you around," said the philosopher. "What happened?"

He explained as best he could.

"So now we know for sure," he summarized as he sat up groggily, "that it was Siriun plotting which set Earth's peoples at each other's throats. We also know, I think, that the Siriuns live in deadly fear of Franklin's gun. Now…" He groaned and held his splitting head in his hands. "…Now our only hope is to build that gun and fiddle around with the tuning until something happens."

"I have built the weapon," interrupted the tech. "It is a very simple adaptation of a radar transmitter. Unfortunately it has a limited range—not over a thousand miles at the outside, I should say."

Merek began pacing the chamber as he had so often paced his cabin out on Sirius… Three steps forward. Turn. Three steps back.

"Iskra," he said at last, "where is Mendez now?"

"Fleet circle 'bout 500 miles up. Leave fo' Beacon soon."

"Can you see Mendez?"

"No seeum. Smellum!" She wrinkled her freckled nose.

"Can you, uh, smell Marian?"

"Marian aw ri'. Cry now. Feel like big foo'."

"Could you get a message to Marian?"

"Try," she shrugged. "Like try tickle stone wit' feather."

"Do your best to reach her. Warn her about Mendez."

Standing with feet widespread, Iskra gripped the platinum rail with both hands until her knuckles shone white. Sweat formed on her forehead, trickled down her cheeks and dripped off her out-thrust chin.

"Mebbe so," she said at last as she relaxed with a sigh.

"Pancrief!" Merek called into his wrist communicator.

"Standing by, sir."

"Big job for you. Land on the reservation. Convince the refugees—some of them, anyway—that Earth's destruction was caused, not by the misuse of machines but by Siriun sabotage. We have evidence here which indicates they feared our race after it developed atomic power and space travel—wanted to stop our expansion."

"Yes sir. It may be difficult under the circumstances. Captain McCarthy died last night—in his sleep."

"Oh… Well, you'll have to try, anyway. We're beginning to crack this nightmare but I have a hunch we won't get far unless the refugees help us."

"I'll do my best. Maybe Sharon will back me up." Pancrief cut off.

"Now," said Merek to Iskra, "tune in Mendez, or whatever you do." To the tech he added, "Start Franklin's weapon and tune it slowly along whatever waveband it uses. If it's directional, aim it at the fleet overhead."

Switches flipped. Tubes glowed. A low humming filled Merek's ears, as though a swarm of bees had entered the room. He shook his head; covered his ears. The humming originated inside his skull.

"Turn off," Iskra wailed, her face white. "Sound like we'en dark start come. No can smell Mendez."

"Then we're stymied again." Merek sat wearily on the nearest chair.

"Here's a suggestion," said Franklin. "Try using the weapon in bursts. Let Iskra check Mendez's reactions between those bursts."

Hours passed as they tinkered. Many of the stampeded Councilors returned shamefacedly to report that the city's hysteria was dying down for lack of new material on which to feed. Someone brought sandwiches and black coffee. Alpha sank below the western horizon and Beta's warm rays began slanting through the chamber's eastern windows. Still Iskra merely shrugged her lovely shoulders after each burst of the Franklin gun.

They worked across the entire spectrum of radiation. At one point Iskra collapsed when they struck the band on which her extrasensory perception functioned. At another all Centaurans in the room became violently ill. But it was not until the vibrations were almost as short as those of light that the girl reported anything extraordinary taking place aboard the flagship.

"Mendez nervous," she whispered after one such blast. "Breath come quick. Stop talk to Rolphson on right beam. Lick lips. Start cigarette. Throw 'way."

They tinkered some more.

"Mendez sweat," said Iskra. "Walk floor. Twist hand. Swear. Send Marian to cabin. Lock in."

The tech whistled through his buck teeth and moved the selector a hair.

"Mendez gone!" cried the girl.

"What do you mean, 'Gone'?" they yelled at her.

"Somethin' else on bridge," she reiterated. "Smell like Mendez. Think like—Siriun!"

"What is it doing?" Poynetz begged.

"Give order. Fleet reform. Head fo' Sirius."

"We're nudging the infra-red," said the tech as he turned the vernier ever so slightly. "Can't go much higher." He turned on the power; held it; cut it.

"Siriun lie across desk," Iskra reported. "Twitch! Officer run. Get doctor."

"What is Marian doing?"

"'Ammer on door. Scream. Try get out. Nobody 'ear. Ship go fas' now," she added wearily. "Eight G. Marian flat on floor. On bridge Siriun in Mendez body wiggle li'l bit. Open eye. Sit up."

"That does it!" Merek beat his forehead with a clenched fist. "The fleet is drawing out of range. When it gets to Sirius we're really done for."

A bell tone from his communicator interrupted.

"Made it, sir," came Pancrief's voice. "I put it to them straight and Sharon backed me to the hilt. I think they had an inkling of the real truth before. Anyway, when Sharon told 'em that if the Siriuns planned to enslave humanity it was better for the refugees to die on their feet than live on their knees, you should have heard 'em cheer. She tore passive resistance to shreds and threw it away. Then she ran up the old United Nations banner on the wreck and asked for volunteers. Practically everyone young enough to walk joined up. What next?"

"Get refugee board ship quick," cried Iskra, who had been eavesdropping. "Pan bring ship 'ere. Pick up Iskra, Merek, Franklin... Go Beacon."

"Are you crazy? Rolphson will crucify us."

"Mus' take chance." She danced up and down like a little girl. "Please, brudder."

"If we could get Rolphson to help and the refugees could handle the controls we still might use the barb drive to beat Mendez to the Dark Planet," Merek mused. "O.K., Pancrief. Take the *Terra* up fast and bring her here. Hover over the Capitol out of reach of the mob. Drop ladders and a baggage sling. Bring all volunteers along, of course."

"Roger," chortled Pancrief.

Briefly the admiral outlined Iskra's wild plan to Franklin, Poynetz and three or four other Councilors.

"It's our last chance," he concluded.

"At least it may give us a breathing spell," said Franklin. "Poynetz, you will take over here while I'm gone. First thing you have to do is to order all Centaurans to go to the Bank and have their confounded memory clocks turned back. Make men and women of them again instead of death-fearing immortals. Then, in case we fail out there, start building defenses for a last-ditch fight here."

"People will be completely lost and helpless without their memories." Poynetz was back in form. "How will they know how to run modern machines and things?"

"They're lost and helpless now." Franklin led the Pizarian to a window and pointed to the milling throngs which surrounded the chamber, waiting for the Council to perform some miracle. "Turn them back, starting with yourself. You had a lot more backbone when I knew you…and were a pretty good soldier as well as a bum philosopher. They'll learn the new techniques quickly if they have to."

"Poynetz goo' man," said Iskra cheerfully as she and Franklin helped the wistful tech carry his jerry-built transmitter to the Capitol's flat roof. "Put backbone in Council, Centauran. Makeum fight." She hitched up her kilt as though getting ready for battle, then grimaced as she thought of her bad arm.

The *Terra* drifted across the screaming city half an hour later to drop a boarding ladder and freight net on the roof. They sent the precious gun up first.

"You'd better go with us," said Merek as the tech turned reluctantly away. "You know how to tune the thing. What is *your* name, by the way?"

"Paulson, sir." The little fellow's face shone. "I'm absolutely non-telepathic, sir. Thank you, sir." He went up the ladder like a monkey.

"Your turn next." Merek turned to Iskra to find tears of vexation in her eyes.

"No can climb," she raged. "Iskra no goo' wit' one arm. Leave behind, be mudder."

"Ahoy, *Terra*," he called. "Drop that net again."

Down it came. Giggling, Iskra curled up inside it like a kitten.

Inside the ship they were surrounded by cheering crew members and young refugees of both sexes.

"Friends," said Merek when he had caught his breath from the climb up the ladder, "we're heading toward Beacon to try to make an alliance with the barbs against the Siriuns. Emperor Rolphson may feed us to the fees. Frankly, we haven't one chance in a thousand for survival. I think that one chance depends on the help you veterans and you refugees give us. But don't let that sway you; if anyone wants to be landed, let him speak up."

No one spoke. Instead, another cheer went up as Merek led the way to the bridge.

"Take over, Iskra," he said when they got there. "I don't want to try maneuvering with the barb drive at such close quarters."

She waited until the anti-gravs had pushed them to a safe distance above the disturbed ant hill which was Mercon City. She squinted; beat time with her foot; studied the starry heavens; pushed the makeshift lever a notch; jerked it back as the ship threatened to turn inside out.

Gasping from the wicked agony, the others looked through the view port. Parched Beacon lay under them like a skull; all about floated the barb globes.

"Time Iskra come 'ome," a sardonic voice boomed through the communicator. "Bring Merek, udders 'board flagship. 'Ave talk. Rolphson speak."

A gig was waiting when Merek, Iskra, Pancrief, Franklin and Sharon reached the pressure hatch. A little later they were being marched through the draughty corridors of the emperor's ship to the savage skirling of bagpipes. This time the warriors who formed their escort did not jeer.

Rolphson received them in the same silk-draped, fur-piled room where Merek had renewed acquaintance with his father. The youth had grown to virile manhood in the months which had intervened. He was wide of shoulder and firm of jaw. He winked at them gravely and studied Iskra until Merek felt a pang of jealousy. Then the ruler noted her stiff arm and shrugged, as though writing her off.

After introducing the group of chiefs and chieftainesses who attended him, Rolphson clapped his hands. The inevitable horns of mead and platters of stew were brought in.

"Iskra jus' tell Rolphson 'bout new weapon," the emperor said as the feast got under way. "Centauran want make alliance. Use gun on Siriun?"

The admiral nodded.

"Barb no need Centauran. Take weapon. Use."

"I think not," Merek answered between bites. "Your people fear the Dark. Our gun has only a short range. Barbarians would never be able to get near enough to Sirius to use it. Your pilots would go mad; get lost in the Coal Sack."

The emperor wiped gravy out of his budding mustache and looked long and hard at Sharon while Pancrief ground his teeth. "Rolphson pay refugee much gold to join barb. Guide ship. Aim Franklin gun."

Sharon covered a yawn.

"Give refugee whole planet for 'ome." He drank in her petite, auburn beauty, which was something new in his experience. "Rolphson make Sharon Firs' Mudder."

Sharon laughed.

"Torture?" he suggested.

"Rolphson no talk like Rolph son." Iskra held out her horn for a refill.

"W'at Centauran want?" The emperor flushed and stopped his ragging.

"Simply that your people go back to Omega and leave us in peace if we defeat the Siriuns."

"W'en we start?" Rolphson knew when he was licked.

"At once," Franklin spoke up. "We must beat Mendez to the Dark Planet."

"Refugee no know 'ow run ship," one of the barb chieftains objected.

"I know how," said Sharon proudly. "Many of us understand a bit about space travel. We always feared we might be driven from Mercon as you barbarians were. Our ship is battered, but not quite the wreck we led the Centaurans to believe. My...my father took a lot of us kids on short flights at night and taught us the rudiments of astrogation."

Merek whistled. And he had thought the refugees were children.

"We thought if we refused to use machines and claimed to be non-resistors we might be left in peace," the girl went on. "But not by the Siriuns! None of us are safe in the same universe with them. That's why we consented to help you."

"Sharon think 'round corner like barb." Rolphson patted her shoulder. "Make goo' warrior." To Merek and Franklin he added: "Alliance aw ri'. Wan' sign treaty with blood?"

"Let's drink to victory instead," answered the admiral, who knew the barbs took a dim view of written documents.

Once more the horns were emptied while the fur-kilted clansmen whooped.

"Start now, reach Dark Planet week 'fore Mendez," said Rolphson.

"No goo'," Iskra grunted as she massaged her sword arm. "Siriun send Dark. Centauran no think ri'. Barb go crazy. Run berserk. Kill one 'nudder."

"If there's danger of a mental crackup," said Sharon, "all small arms must be locked up. Then it will take at least a day or two for us refugees to familiarize ourselves with the controls of your ships. Finally, all of you barbs must consent to be confined to quarters until we get within Franklin-gun range of the Dark Planet."

Rolphson looked bleak. The chiefs, who always slept with weapons under their hard pillows, cried out in protest. But they remembered all too vividly the chaos which resulted when the Dark invaded their brains. After a stormy argument during which they almost came to blows, they sullenly agreed to Sharon's ultimatum.

"Also," said Franklin, "we can't start until each ship is equipped with one of my weapons. "If that is done we may be able to deploy our forces on landing and attack several...uh...cities simultaneously."

"Cities!" jeered Pancrief, who had kept glumly silent all through the conference. "How do we know the Siriuns live in cities? How do we know they live at all, in the accepted sense? Maybe they're just ghosts pawing at our minds."

"Why Pan!" Sharon's eyes widened. "You're not suggesting we don't attack?"

"Oh, I'm for an attack all right," he grumbled, "but I do like to see what

I'm attacking. Searchlights won't be any good beyond a few yards in that muck… Say, Merek!" He chewed a bony knuckle. "How about a bunch of direct-view sniperscopes? The Siriuns couldn't fog them… Nuh-huh. The barbs could never make enough of them in such a short time, especially if they have to turn out Franklin guns too."

"Pancrief show how. Barb do!" Rolphson bristled.

"O.K." Pan dropped an eyelid at Merek. "Take me to your lab, if you have one, and we'll get busy."

CHAPTER XV

Rolphson made good his boast, his artificers sweating over their hand forges like demons for 48 straight hours to do the job. When his fleet lifted from sun-scorched Beacon three days after that first conference, each ship was equipped with unbeautiful but workable and portable radiators, while a goodly supply of 'scopes was stored—along with racked swords and hand weapons—in their locked and refugee-guarded armories.

With other refugees at their helms, the battlewagons smashed their way through the continuum along an impossible trajectory plotted by barbarian astrogators. Before their crews had time to draw three choking breaths they had hurdled the light years and materialized in normal space, 5000 miles or less from the Dark Planet.

The three Centaurans were standing with Iskra on the *Terra's* bridge when Sharon jerked them out of hyperspace like a veteran. As they fought the nausea resulting from that fantastic hop they stared at their target. It shone like a great pearl in the crude light of mammoth Sirius and its white-dwarf twin.

"What fools we are," said Merek bitterly. "Sirius has been the evil genius of the human race for countless millennia. Now here we are, at our rope's end, attacking it with a...a fly swatter!"

"Isn't it about time?" Sharon asked matter-of-factly as she watched other barb ships popping into view like balls in some sleight-of-hand trick. As a tribute to her father she was wearing his threadbare old United Nations uniform today. With her red hair and freckled, eager face, she looked cute enough to frame.

"The Sumerians feared the Dog Star as a bringer of storms, heat and swarms of locusts," Franklin recalled, to hide the depression which was clamping down on him. "The Greeks said Sirius was the vicious dog of that hunter of the skies, Orion."

"Father always said Orion was the only Irishman in the heavens," Sharon quipped.

"Homer called Sirius the Evil Star." This from Merek as he leaned dispiritedly against the thick plexiglass of the blister. "The Romans sacrificed red dogs to avert pestilence during the Dies Caniculares, or Dog Days."

"Wish we had a few red dogs to sacrifice right now," muttered Pancrief.

"I have a hunch we'll have our ears beaten off when we go downstairs."

"Pan!" Sharon's voice was sharp. "What has got into you?"

"Nothing," he frowned. Then his own voice sharpened. "Watch out, Sharon! You'll collide with that ship to our left!"

"What ship?"

"That one right there!" Pancrief lunged toward the controls.

"Stay away!" Sharon snatched an automatic from the control desk and pointed it unwaveringly. "That ship is at least ten miles distant."

Pancrief's Adam's apple bobbed. "Guess you're right," he mumbled. "I thought... My head..."

"Get off the bridge, both of you," Merek yelled in unreasoning anger. "Who's in command here, anyway? I'll take over now, Sharon. It's going to be ticklish getting through those clouds."

"Sorry." Sharon's voice was tight as her grip on the gun. "Stay where you are!"

A spitting ball of insensate fury launched itself across the room. It was Iskra gone berserk, driven by screaming blood lust toward the first object in her path.

Caught off-balance by the unprovoked attack, Sharon fired wildly, then went down under the barbarian's rush, fighting to protect her eyes from wildly jabbing fingers.

Jerked out of their funk by the hellish scene, the others sprang to her rescue.

Although she had only one good arm, the thing that had been Iskra fought like a demon, biting, punching, digging at exposed nerve endings with fingertips of steel. Almost, she succeeded in crippling all of them.

Hating himself for what he had to do, Merek managed to catch the berserker's stiff arm and twist it with all his might.

Something gave. Iskra collapsed with a wild scream.

Working like men in a bad dream while battered little Sharon dragged herself back to the controls, the others bound Iskra, then set about reviving her.

"Dark," she moaned like a child as consciousness returned. "Dark say... 'OOOooo... Kill Sharon... Bring ship down... Surrender... OOOooo...'"

She struggled to a sitting position and opened eyes into which the light of sanity was slowly returning. "Iskra 'urt bad," she whimpered and buried her bruised, dirt-streaked face in her hands.

"Iskra—Iskra, honey," Merek pleaded as he knelt beside her. "Forgive me." Then, as he realized what had happened, he whooped: "Iskra! Look! You're using your right arm! The lesions were broken loose in that fight!"

She raised her head; stared at her fingers; flexed them experimentally. A great joy was born on her face.

"Use both arm," she husked. "Iskra goo' 'nuff for Merek 'gain!" To prove it, she threw those arms around her blood brudder and kissed him until his lips ached.

"Look outside!" Pancrief's cry broke the idyll. "Something awful's happening."

Merek lifted Iskra to the blister just in time to see the nearest ship explode in a flash of atomic fire. Farther away, a second vessel was falling apart like a badly-constructed tinker toy. As they stared, two others winked back into hyper.

"Barb go crazy." Iskra had that far-away look in her eyes. "Kill refugee wit' bare 'ands on four ship. Seize bridge."

"What about Rolphson's flagship?" came Sharon's frantic cry. In her excitement she had jammed the communicator switches and was getting nothing but a roar of static. "Merek, call Paulson and get him to start the radio working."

"Flagship aw ri'," Iskra reported. "Refugee 'old bridge. Same on udder ship."

Paulson scurried in, tinkered and shook his mousey head.

"Whatever the Siriuns are sending up has jinxed the radio, sir."

"Use the blinker then," Merek ordered. "Tell all the ships to turn on their Franklin guns and get down within their range quick!"

"I've been thinking," Franklin said to nobody in particular as he ran nervous fingers through his white hair. "Merek said once that when the Dark came to Omega it short-circuited many types of radiation. Lights dimmed. Heating units cooled. Well, since my radiator is powered by electricity…"

"No think! No think!" Iskra shrieked. "Siriun 'ear."

By reflex action, Sharon slammed home the switch of the *Terra's* Franklin gun. Even as she did so the gibbering Dark hit them with vastly augmented force.

"Done for this time…and all my fault," sobbed Franklin as the ship's lights dimmed and the gun panel ammeter, which had started to climb, sagged back. Merek and Pancrief were weeping like schoolboys. Iskra was frothing at the mouth and tearing at her bonds. Only Sharon and non-telepathic Paulson remained calm as they nursed the staggering ship.

Gradually the lights brightened, the ammeter needle snapped back across its dial and the buzzing whine of the Franklin gun steadied.

"Thank God we made it before the Siriuns caught on," whispered Sharon. The others bowed their heads.

"Two more ships going down out of control," Paulson reported. "The others got the guns going in time to save themselves. We're not licked yet."

"They'll pay for this," Pancrief raged as he dried his tears. "No slimy Siriun is going to get away with making me blubber."

"How do you feel now, Iskra?" Merek inquired, as he mopped his own streaming face.

"Fine!" She took a long shuddering breath. "Gun' push Dark back. Dark go 'ere; go dere. Like scare'." She yawned prodigiously. "…Iskra sleep now. Tire'." Her eyelids fluttered shut. She was asleep before he finished untying her.

CHAPTER XVI

As his mind cleared, Merek felt a new spirit of exhilaration surge through him. The prospect of battle warmed his blood. His mind dismissed the hazards, the unknowables that lay ahead.

"How many ships still with us?" he asked Paulson.

"Eighteen, sir, including this one." The C.O. looked up briefly from the now perfectly-operating radio. "All of them in fighting shape except the *Montrak*. Her refugee pilot—Fortune's his name, sir—says the *Montrak's* Franklin gun is partially jammed. Her barbs are still in a bad way."

"Tell Captain Fortune to drop back out of range. Tell him to cover our rear and try to warn us in case Mendez and his fleet arrive before we have finished downstairs."

He looked at Iskra. The thought of his incubus-ridden enemy spoiled some of his new confidence. Perhaps she could make contact... He shook his head as he studied her wan, sleeping face. Don't disturb her yet. She might be able to help more later on if she had a chance to rest now. Perhaps, he ventured to hope, Mendez had got himself lost in hyperspace.

"You had better take the controls now," said Sharon. "I'm afraid I'm not up to making a landing. Meantime, I have a request to make."

"You name it," he said absent-mindedly as he stepped to the board, his mind busy with calculations of fire power, moves that might be anticipated from the Siriuns, principles of tactics and strategy remembered from his reading about old battles and his own experience.

"Food," Sharon replied. "We refugees cling to that old-fashioned habit of eating three times a day. And the McCarthys are among the best cling-ers in the clan. After what the barbs have been through, I suspect they're hungry too."

Merek had a flash of resentment. Food indeed! Why couldn't the refu-gees employ the C.S.N. technique of swallowing delayed-action concen-trates before going into battle—the technique which made it unnecessary to carry bulky food and cooling equipment on short campaigns, and freed all hands for uninterrupted action? Instead, he was stuck with hundreds of refugees and thousands of barbs who wouldn't be worth much as fighters until they had square meals under their belts... Oh well, this was far from being one of the galaxy's ten best-organized expeditions.

"Go ahead," he grinned belatedly at Sharon. "It will take us at least three hours to surface. I'll pass the word along to the rest of the fleet. The rest of you go along to the mess hall, too. I can handle things here for a while. Eat hearty." He clamped his teeth on an impulse to add that it might be the last meal for all of them.

Alone with the heavily-sleeping Iskra, Merek swallowed three food capsules, paced the bridge and tried to think. A sense of the foolhardiness of the venture re-assailed him. There were sketchy reports in War College archives about Siriun conquest of several neighboring solar systems, but none defined their weapons or strategies. It was even rumored they never employed fighting ships.

"Never employed fighting ships!" The phrase lingered in his mind, inviting analysis as he plotted a new orbit for the *Terra*, swung her into it with a short burst of rudder tubes and called the coordinates to the rest of the fleet. Did the Siriuns depend mainly on engendering fear and blind terror by their telepathic broadcasting? And what conceivable means could they use to broadcast thoughts? "I've got to think this thing through," he muttered. "Got to!"

He was still pacing when the others returned. There was no need for orders. Sharon took her place beside the controls. Pancrief methodically checked the infra-red gun pointers. Paulson called one after the other of the commanding barb officers and their refugee pilots and logged their reports. Franklin stood at the blister, watching the featureless planet as it came up to meet them.

The admiral paused long enough to switch on the battle perception record which would give them—if they ever got back—a detailed summary of action during the forthcoming battle. What kind of battle and what form of action, he wondered. Action without Siriun fighting ships? Was that haunting phrase a clue to understanding of conditions he would have to face within the next—he glanced at the chronometer—the next 59 minutes?

The Siriuns had vast powers, he thought, still trying to pin down that elusive concept. They could engender fear—fear which could kill barbarians or drive them mad; fear which could cause radio static or short circuit an electric light; fear which could bring proud Centaurans crawling to the Dark Planet as envoys of appeasement.

But how did they generate that power; engender that fear? No fighting ships! By projecting their thoughts? Yes! But a thought is a feeble thing; much like a radio wave. You could build a receiver with a relay which would put out a light if actuated by feeble radio wave. But here was a thought transmitter which actuated not only a receiver—the brain—but acted directly on insensate matter! No, he corrected himself: Not matter: just other types of radiation such as light or electricity. Then you had to have a powerful, an ultra-powerful transmitter which would warp not only thought but the whole field of radiation across thousands of miles of empty space. And such a transmitter…

"Fifty-three minutes before we level at ten miles," Sharon called. Her voice seemed calm but Merek sensed overtones of panic.

"Fifty-three. Fifty-two. Fifty-one. Fifty." The unspoken words ticked louder and louder in his brain. "I need more time than that," he cried inwardly. "I must have more time! I can't think this thing through in forty-nine minutes. I can't. I can't!"

"What's our plan of attack, sir?" This time it was Pancrief who spoke. "The other ships are asking for instructions. I've told them you're waiting till the last possible minute but they're getting uneasy." The Pizarian hesitated. Then came the words Merek dreaded, yet knew would come—the words that no officer but Pancrief would have dared utter: "You have a plan, don't you, sir?"

Merek felt the perspiration break out on his forehead, his neck, the backs of his hands. He was the leader of this tattered charge against the enemies of civilization. The peoples of Centaurus and Omega had put their last trust and hope in him. So had Iskra, Sharon, Franklin, Pancrief and his handful of veterans and refugee volunteers.

And he had no plan!

He fought back the impulse to tell Pancrief the truth: that he was lost in a labyrinth of thought leading nowhere; that they were all lost with him in the cruel, seductive fog which already was beginning to brush its wet fingers along the *Terra's* ports.

"We will rendezvous according to normal operational practice in 48 minutes," he said in a matter-of-fact voice. "Tell the other ships that. We will follow a very simple plan which they can all understand as soon as the *Terra* initiates it. For purposes of deception, that is all that can be said about our attack plan now."

"My great twinkling stars!" he said to himself as Pancrief began relaying the message. "I sounded as bombastic as old Mendez himself."

To warriors like myself, speculated the cornered admiral as he resumed his pacing, armies and navies are the only sources of military power. In the last analysis, armed might is employed to inspire fear in our enemies…fear that will make them quit fighting and surrender. But, so far as we can prove, the Siriuns do not have armies and navies. Yet they inspire fear. How? By means of thought power multiplied almost to infinity by some sort of telepathic transmitter. Destroy that transmitter…b*ut first, find that transmitter.*

But how could such a thing be located on a planet containing God knew how many million square miles of surface and wrapped in a twenty-mile-thick cloud blanket? If there were such a thing as telepathic radar… Or was there such a thing? Maybe so. Mebbe so, as Iskra would say… Iskra!

"Thirty-seven minutes!" Sharon's panic was no longer hidden.

"Iskra, honey!" He knelt beside the sleeping girl and shook her gently.

"Iskra tir'," she murmured, stirring fretfully. "Go 'way."

"Iskra! I need your help again." There was no response.

"Thirty-six minutes!"

"Iskra 'fraid," he jabbed at her in the patois, striving to reach her subconscious mind. "Merek say rabbit no fight. Subchief Rabbit Clan 'fraid to fight too!"

She awoke, fighting mad, just as he had hoped.

"Listen, honey." He caught her fist as she swung it at his head. "Remember I told the Council there was one chance in a thousand that we could slow up the Siriuns? Now I think there's a chance in a hundred that we can stop them for good. That's worth a fight, isn't it?"

"Yah!" Her anger evaporated.

"You may get hurt again. You may be killed."

"Dat aw ri'. W'at Brudder Merek want Iskra do?"

Merek motioned to Pancrief to join them, then continued: "I'm going to gamble everything on one big guess. I'm guessing that somewhere on the Dark Planet is a super-transmitter, a tremendously powerful mechanical device that can magnify and send out telepathic waves on a tight beam.

"So we've got to locate that transmitter and move in fast," Merek continued, one eye on the clock. "Iskra is the only one who can do it for us, at least on this ship. And I don't want to toss any guesses at Rolphson just yet, or," he added thoughtfully, "at Siriun eavesdroppers."

"How do you know there's only one transmitter?" asked the practical Pizarian.

"I don't. But in view of its long range, I'm betting the equipment required is so tremendous that there won't be more than two of them at the most. Since the possible second one would broadcast in the opposite direction from its twin it must be on the other side of the planet where it can't harm us. We can attend to it later."

"And you think Iskra can get you a fix on the thing?"

"Iskra get fix," the girl said confidently. "Fix Siriun too."

"It won't be nice." Merek knew she understood what he had in mind.

"Dat aw ri'. On Omega rabbit chase fox." She was impish and gay. Lying with long straight legs together and hands held rigidly at her sides she added, "Tie Iskra now. Might make mistake w'en Dark come... Chase Merek!"

"We'll hold the other ships back slightly," Merek explained as he and Pancrief did her bidding. "Then we'll warp the *Terra* into a series of what used to be called 'lazy eights.' We'll move back and forth, descending slowly, over the part of the planet facing us. Iskra will give us a series of directional readings on the waves as she picks them up."

"But Iskra can only hear the Siriuns if we turn off the Franklin gun."

"So we'll turn it off for short periods, the way we did when we were putting the bee on Mendez's incubus."

"No," said Franklin, who could not fail to hear the conversation, "it won't work. If you shut off the gun, that transmitter down below will short-circuit every piece or apparatus on board. You won't be able to get the gun started again and the *Terra* will crash. Why... Why..." He pressed his hand to the bid wound on his scalp. "I remember now. That's why the lifeboat hit that mine. We were drifting...out of control... I heard Hank shouting..."

"Thirty-three minutes," Sharon exclaimed. "We've got to do something right now. Would this do...? Cut down the power on the gun but don't stop it? Iskra should be able to..."

"That's it. That's it!" Merek leaped to the mike and issued the "hold back" order to the other ships. Paulson knelt beside Iskra, electronic computer at his elbow. Pancrief gripped the power knob of the Franklin gun and started turning it counter-clockwise.

"Hear anything, Iskra?" he asked. When she shook her head, he reduced the wattage still more. The buzzing of the gun dwindled. The bridge lights dimmed slightly. The ship staggered as one of its drive tubes sputtered, and went into a shallow dive. "'Ear now." Iskra bit her lips. "Not strong. Say: 'Oooo. Aw Centauran stupid. Be trap down below... Made think like Siriun.' Say: 'OOOoooo. Barb make goo' fee food.' Say..." She writhed in her cocoon of plastic cord.

"What's our speed, Sharon?" snapped Merek, steadying himself by gripping a handhold as the ship lurched.

"Thousand mph. Altitude 21 miles," she sang out calmly. "Losing both altitude and speed fast."

"Thought get stronger," Iskra cried in a voice which made the little group shiver. "Stronger...darker...s*tronger*!" She began to babble a series of revolting, insane threats in a wild effusion of anguish. Veins stood out on her forehead. The cords of her neck flexed and glistened with sweat. She fought her bonds like a madwoman and ground her teeth until a red trickle ran from her mouth.

Transfixed by the sight of the torture he had ordered, Merek waited helplessly for the peak of it to pass. He had witnessed the agonies of death on battlefields of four planets but never had he seen, or himself endured, a thing like this. Every moment he expected the girl to break—to burn herself out like a worn-out tritium tube. Instead she clung to consciousness of a sort, vibrating with a spark that seemed to invite the full play of the mighty currents which wracked her. At last she partially relaxed and opened eyes which were still sane. She tried to speak but she could only croak.

"Did you chart that?" Merek gritted at the tech.

"Yes sir." The little fellow was sniffling shamelessly. "But it will take at least three more runs to get a real fix."

"Speed 630," sobbed Sharon. "Altitude ten miles and a bit."

"Full power on the gun, Pan," he ordered. "Bring her up to speed and altitude again, Sharon. We'll come in at right angles to our first run this time."

As they obeyed, the *Terra* hit her stride again. Soon the fog, which had been pressing against the blister like a pall, began to disperse as they climbed back into the harsh light of Sirius.

Twice more the *Terra* stumbled around its lazy eight above the planet. Twice more Iskra went bravely through that awful cycle.

"Got it, sir!" Paulson whimpered at last as the calculator whirred and chattered its answer to their riddle. "There seem to be three beams, one aimed at Centaurus, one at Omega and the other at the fleet. They all come from a spot that can't be more than two miles square. Here are the coordinates." He scribbled on a sheet of plascript and handed it to Merek. "Wait. I'll put the time on that."

"Great Galaxy!" his commander gasped. "Twelve minutes left. Pancrief! Tell the others we level off and rendezvous at this spot. Altitude ten miles. Attack formation."

"Do we surround the transmitting area and work toward the center?" The Pizarian already was at the mike.

"No. I'm afraid of what the Franklin guns might do to our own minds if any ship got caught in a cross fire. I'll take the *Terra* off toward the center. Have the others follow in single file. They know the order. There's bound to be some tremendous contraption down there which will show up in the sniperscopes. We'll go into a tight circle. Fire at will in…ten minutes, thirty seconds. Don't ask for acknowledgments. We haven't time."

"And if," said Pancrief when he had broadcast the message, "the infrared cannon doesn't do the job. What then?"

"We'll crash-land and go after them with hand weapons."

"Dat goo'," sighed Iskra weakly. "Iskra wanna use sword arm 'gain."

She sat up groggily as Merek untied her and began chafing her swollen wrists and ankles.

"No," he said. "You've done far more than your share. You'll stay right here and rest this time, my lady."

"Dat w'at Merek think," she answered cheerfully.

"What kind of a crazy war is this?" groaned Pancrief. Nevertheless, he was grinning broadly as he and Paulson continued to flash coded instructions which got the other ships lined up behind the *Terra*, with their crews lashed down in shock harness for the possible crash-landings.

In the few minutes remaining, Merek checked with his own deck of-ficers—forgotten men in this type of pushbutton warfare—and found time to promise all on board that they would get their whack at the hated Siriuns soon. Then he took over the controls from Sharon and, his eyes glued to the sniperscope, sent the *Terra* screaming down through the thickening fog toward her unseen target.

"This is it, rabbit," he smiled tightly at Iskra, as a faint "beep" and a twinkle of purple light on the indicator panel showed that the assembled fleet was following him down.

CHAPTER XVII

"Trouble!" said Pancrief at the communicator as he clapped both hands over his earphones as though to hear better. "Double trouble!"

"What?" Merek did not dare take his eyes from the illuminated chart on which the *Terra* was a white dot racing toward a rendezvous with a spot marked X.

"Franklin's damned guns are heterodyning in this tight formation—canceling each other out. At least that's the way it sounds."

"Well?"

"Pilot Horton—he's on the ship right behind us—says his barbs have cut loose again. They're battering down the diaphragm to the bridge. Crazy as loons… Oh, oh! Ship Number Three is out of formation. Ships Seven and Eight have collided! God, what a mess!" He snatched off the phones as though they were burning him and hurled them across the cabin. "What a foul, misbegotten mess, just when we had 'em in our pocket."

Merek risked a glance at Iskra, expecting her to be creeping toward him like a tigress. Instead she was standing wide-eyed with horror at this unexpected development.

"Why aren't we getting the effect?" he yelled at Franklin.

"I… I can't imagine," the president quavered.

"I think it's because we're in the lead," cried Paulson. "The others are in that crossfire you were worried about."

"Then it's up to us," gritted Merek. "We'll lead from weakness instead of from strength. Get our infra-reds warmed up. We're going in. Tell the others to follow us if they can. If they can't, they should break formation and get out of range."

"On target in ten seconds," warned Sharon, who had not lifted her eyes from the chart.

"Hold on, everybody," said Pancrief, shifting quickly to the gun pointer. "Something's showing on the 'scope. But what it is the devil himself couldn't guess. Damn this rarefield pitch outside."

Five seconds. Four seconds. Even though their Franklin guns still functioned properly, the Siriun broadcast was getting through this short range. The ship's lights turned blood red, and her controls were erratic. Iskra was screaming thinly. Even Merek's brain was whirling so he could barely see the chart. He turned away from it in synthetic despair and did not even notice that Sharon had leaped to take his place.

Three seconds. Two seconds. Pancrief collapsed at the gun pointer and sprawled across Franklin's senseless body. Paulson, the non-telepath, snatched the triggers and held them steady as rocks.

One second.

The *Terra* bucked like a fee as her three old infra-reds let loose. Sucking power like sponges from the ship's generators and packs they sprayed toward the invisible target a roaring, boiling, short-range burst of radiation beside which the fires of hell paled to moonbeams. Against the tremendous armament of the Centauran flagship, the *Terra* would have been able to last for seconds only. Now her guns belched on and on. And, Merek saw as he leaned his throbbing head against the blister, eight of the remaining barbarian ships followed suit.

In the center of this maelstrom a giant's finger pointed accusingly at the attackers—a finger of steel which, as the endless moments passed turned cherry red, then white, then burst into a flame which outshone that of the guns above as the giant slowly folded his finger back against his palm. And then…

S-i-l-e-n-c-e!

Cool, beautiful, crystal clear silence. Silence so vibrant it could be heard. Silence that took one's breath away. The lovely, much-sought cone of silence that, since man first let radio waves guide him, had meant safety to generations of navigators and astrogators. No. It was even more than that. It was a peace beyond human understanding, at least since the Siriuns had started their hellish broadcasting across the galaxy.

"We'll go down to two hundred feet," said Merek, fighting to keep his voice even. "Paulson, crisscross an area ten miles square just to be sure. Pancrief," he added as the shamefaced Pizarian staggered erect, "tell the other ships which followed us in, to land when we do and get ready for a sally. Try to get the remaining ships here too. Tell Fortune to keep a sharp lookout for Mendez. We're not out of the woods yet. And," he added as his friend started to open his big mouth, "don't apologize for fainting. The Siriuns knocked me right out of the ring too."

They did not need the 'scope now to show them a job well done. Beneath them, glowing through the gloom, lay the metallic skeleton of what undoubtedly had been the tallest tower in the entire galaxy. More than a mile high, it must have been. Spotted irregularly near the fallen giant were other glowing objects—difficult to identify, but resembling flattened globes and cylinders. Probably the sources of power for the obscene carrier wave which had been modulated by the even more fiendish thoughts of the Siriuns.

Two hours later they finished their second scorching of the area. Merek was about to give the landing order to the *Terra* and the sixteen barb ships which had finally assembled when the alarm on the radar clanged.

"Patrols!" cried Pancrief. "We caught them napping but I knew they'd finally catch up with us. Here we go again."

"A barrel of Scopio says they're not Siriun patrols," Merek frowned. "Look at that screen!"

"It's the fleet," Pancrief whispered, licking his well-chewed lips. "Dozens of pips. Clap hands, here comes Mendez. And here goes what's left of us."

Catching a twinkle in Iskra's eyes, Merek played a hunch.

"Tune in the communicator," he ordered briskly, "and invite Rear Admiral Mendez down for tea."

It was not Mendez but a greatly puzzled Marian whose face appeared on the screen.

"Admiral Mendez had a nervous breakdown of some kind about two hours ago," she began without preamble. "He's conscious now but seems to have amnesia. He can't remember a thing which happened after he made that first treaty with Sirius."

"That's too bad. Can he explain why he brought the fleet here this time?"

"Hasn't the faintest idea. He even denies he locked me in my cabin… When he collapsed, one of the officers let me out and of course I took over immediately."

"Of course." What on Mercon, thought Merek, had he ever seen in this dry-as-dust creature? But then, that had been before she had gone through the Memory Bank wringer which she had devised in spite of Iskra's warning. Studying her wan, unutterably remote face Merek knew that he was looking, not at a warm and troubled woman but at a human thinking machine.

"Come on down, Your Intelligence," he said gently. "We have just conquered the Dark Planet. I'll explain about Mendez and everything. Contact Pilot Horton. He will guide you to our landing place."

* * * *

It was a disappointed but still uneasy collection of humans and near-humans who set foot on the Siriun planet for the first time ten hours later. (Scout ships had returned to the fleet in the meantime without finding the slightest sign of organized opposition or even of life on the entire fogbound sphere.) Clocks said it was morning, but there was only the faintest lightening of the mist blanket.

First came an armored halftrack bearing Marian and leaders of the joint expedition. (Rolphson at first had insisted on riding a fee, but the usually fearless insect had crouched trembling in its cage and refused to be enticed from it, even by the smell of blood.) Then, in order of precedence, came the refugees who alone had made success possible; the swaggering veteran crew of the *Terra*; the battered, edgy barbarians and, in the rear, the pop-eyed landing crews carried by ships of the Centauran fleet.

Looking like monsters, with the upper halves of their faces covered by protruding snout-like sniper scopes, they left the well-guarded ships behind. Weapons in hand, they passed the still-smoking wreck of the tele-pathic projector and advanced warily toward what the scouts had described as a population center of some sort nearby.

First they crossed a marshy plain which was scattered with black boul-ders—at least they looked black through the 'scopes—and broken here and there by the eroded fangs of ancient hills. After slipping and sliding for half an hour in the sucking mud they entered the ruins of what must have been, in some other age, a magnificent city.

"Ruins!" puzzled Merek as he stopped the car and peered through the gloom. "Our infra-reds didn't touch this territory. Why *ruins* on what was, until yesterday, the richest and most powerful planet in the galaxy?"

"Looks like a civilization in the last stages of decay," whispered Frank-lin, as though afraid the very fog could hear him. "These buildings must have crumbled ages and ages ago."

Fighting a desire to huddle together, they drove on through the swirl-ing mist. They must have gone a mile or more over the broken, rust-rutted streets without finding a single sign of life or a building fit for habitation.

At last, however, one structure in some state of repair loomed across their path like a squat toad. It was unutterably loathsome in its ugliness and yet it exuded a sort of forlorn grandeur. Somewhere far, far inside it, a bell was tolling.

Something stirred in Merek's memory—a snatch of ancient terrestrial poetry he had stumbled across in a dog-eared book. He spoke it softly.

> "*What in the midst lay but the Tower itself?*
> *The round squat turret, blind as the fool's heart,*
> *Built of brown stone, without a counterpart*
> *In the whole world...*"

Franklin picked up the measure:

> "*Not see? because of night perhaps?—*
> *Why, day Came back again for that!...*
> *The hills, like giants at a hunting, lay—*
> *Chin upon hand, to see the game at bay—*
> *Now stab and end the creature—to the heft!*"

He hesitated and Merek went on :

"Not hear? when noise was everywhere? it tolled
Increasing like a bell. Names in my ears,
Of all the lost adventurers my peers—
How such a one was strong, and such was bold,
And such was fortunate, yet each of old
Lost, lost! one moment knelled the woe of years."

"How does it end?" Sharon begged as silence fell again, except for the endless tolling of the unseen bell. She was clinging to Pancrief's arm, in near-panic for the first time since she had joined them. Merek went on slowly:

"I saw them and I knew them all. And yet
Dauntless the slug-horn to my lips I set
And blew, 'Childe Roland to the Dark Tower came.'"

"Slug-horn," grunted Pancrief as he patted his sweetheart's hand. "Our infra-reds slugged them all right. Here we humans are, at the Dark Tower after countless millennia of struggle, agony and failure—and the Tower is dead."

"No," said Iskra. "Siriun not aw dead. Iskra 'ear voice far, far 'way, say: 'OOOooo. Please no kill Siriun, human.' Say: 'OOO-ooo. Long time 'go Dark Plant use up aw iron, coal, oil, udder resource. Fair young, strong race on rich planet. Fear death. 'Ave only mind. Wit' las' steel build telepath transmitter. Make big fear aw over galaxy. Divide an' rule. Make udder planet pay tribute, build ship, grow trade stuff fo' Siriun.'"

"That's enough," snarled Merek. "Tell them they can come in and surrender unconditionally or stay out there and starve."

Iskra resumed singsong: "Say: 'OOOooo. 'Uman goo' after aw. No kill Siriun. Now Siriun not 'fraid be goo' too.'"

Merek doubled up with bitter laughter—laughter that left him weak, shaken, and a wiser man.

"So throughout all the ages," he gasped at last, "the only thing either men or Siriuns have had to fear was fear itself."

"Mebbe so," answered Iskra wistfully, "but w'at Iskra do with sword arm now?"

Ignoring the others in the halftrack, Merek showed her.